Winning Back the Princess

WINNING BACK THE
Princess

A ROYAL SECRETS ROMANCE

WINNING
BACK THE
Princess

A ROYAL SECRETS ROMANCE

USA TODAY BESTSELLING AUTHOR
LINDZEE ARMSTRONG

Snowflake
Press

"Love is a game that two can play and both can win."
—*Eva Gabor*

Chapter One

*P*rincess Charlotte of Durham didn't want to be a special guest at her ex-boyfriend's South African hotel. But being a princess usually meant not getting her way.

She stared out the window of her rented sedan at the magnificent marula trees rushing past, awe racing through her despite her attempts to hold it back. Sparse branches topped with a canopy of green leaves reached toward fluffy white clouds set against the bluest sky she'd ever seen. The narrow road they drove on looked newly resurfaced, and the dark of the blacktop contrasted sharply with the gold grasses on either side. Heat shimmered in the air, and for the first time in her life Charlotte understood what people meant when they talked about desert mirages. The road looked wet, like it had rained recently, but she'd been in the car for more than an hour and there hadn't been a drop of moisture.

Adam had spoken for hours about South Africa, describing everything from the animals to the food while they cuddled together in a hammock on his private rooftop garden. His passion for the country, and the resort he ran there, had come through in every sentence. Had that really only been six weeks ago?

Well, his words hadn't done this country justice. Not surprising, since Adam was a total liar.

Emma reached across the seat and squeezed Charlotte's hand. The cousins were only a few months apart in age and had grown up more like sisters after Emma's parents died in a car crash and she moved to the palace with her brother. Right now, Emma's expressive blue eyes were dark with concern. "Are you okay?"

Charlotte forced a smile and nodded. "Of course. Just admiring the landscape. I can't believe we've let the boys handle the overseas engagements for so long."

"I know." Emma rested her hands primly in her lap. She'd worn a fitted white blazer and skirt today. It made her tanned skin glow and really set off her dark silky hair. "But the family dynamic is changing. Now that Alex and Stefan are occupied with their fiancées, maybe Aunt Nicolette will let us do more solo engagements."

"I hope so." Charlotte's mother was fiercely protective and had preferred to keep the girls close to home. In fact, this was the first time Emma and Charlotte had been allowed out of the country without one of their brothers accompanying them. It was a refreshing change.

"Are you sure you're okay?" Emma pursed her lips, frowning. "I know this is a lot."

In the front seat of the car, Joseph—one of Charlotte's two bodyguards—shifted, murmuring something to the driver in a low voice that she couldn't discern. Joseph was a hulking man, with a stern expression and deep love for firearms. And while he and Karla, Charlotte's female bodyguard who rode in the sedan in front of theirs, were great at keeping confidences, Charlotte still liked to maintain as much privacy as possible.

She leaned closer to Emma, lowering her voice. "Stop acting like I'll fall apart when I see him. I'm not here because of that." She'd only spent ten days with Adam—a whirlwind romance—while he dealt with an issue at one of the Durham hotel properties. No one but Charlotte's security detail and Emma had known about the relationship, which had been fine by Charlotte. After seeing the media circus her brothers Alex and Stefan had gone through, she'd been content to hide the truth.

It had been obvious from the start that Adam wasn't looking for something serious. Charlotte wasn't either, at least at first. But despite her better judgment, she'd fallen hard. And after that last magical evening together, she'd thought maybe he'd fallen for her, too.

"Okay, okay." Emma held up a placating hand. "This isn't about Adam."

"It isn't," Charlotte insisted. "I never would have come if Education Beyond Borders hadn't asked me to keynote at the conference."

She hadn't wanted to say yes to the invitation, considering that this year the three-day education conference was being held at Adam's hotel. That meant Charlotte would probably run into him at least once or twice, which would be beyond uncomfortable. But she'd never been able to refuse an opportunity to speak about the vital importance of education. Since Emma loved traveling, she'd offered to accompany Charlotte for moral support.

Was it too much to hope that Adam wouldn't be at the hotel at all during the conference? Although they'd parted with no promises of the future, she'd thought he'd at least call. Had been so certain he felt the same way she did.

But he hadn't called. First one day had passed, then two, then three. On day five, she'd seen a picture of him with Brionna Cartwright on an online gossip site.

Apparently, the two heirs to hotel fortunes were dating. Charlotte really had been nothing more than a fling.

The pain had gone much deeper than hurt pride.

Her fingers curled around the romance novel she held in her lap, seeking the comfort only a book could bring. If she ran into Adam, she'd treat him like any other employee she encountered on the trip—polite but aloof. She wouldn't think about how his lips could command hers with a simple touch, how soft his hair felt beneath her fingers, the way his mere presence could make her shiver—

Joseph shifted in the front seat, distracting Charlotte. Emma stared at her with a knowing expression.

Charlotte squirmed uncomfortably, pretending to take interest in a rodent scurrying across the road. They had to be mere minutes away from the resort by now.

"You don't have to speak to him," Emma said finally. "Don't even look at him. Pretend he's not there."

Charlotte rolled her eyes. "So if he shows up and tries to talk to me, I'm supposed to just ignore him and walk away? Mother will love that. Very royal behavior."

Emma lifted a shoulder in a shrug. "You're a princess of Durham. You can behave however you'd like, and Adam Montgomery will just have to deal with it."

Charlotte's mouth quirked up in a smile. "It's precisely because I'm a princess that I can't act like that. But thanks for the sentiment all the same. What would I do without you?"

"Be totally overrun by your brothers, probably," Emma said with a laugh.

"Probably." Charlotte sighed, smoothing a hand over the cover of her book. "Maybe we'll get lucky and he won't be here. For all I know, he's off at some other exotic hotel with Little Miss Perfect. They only own about a billion resorts across the globe between the two of them."

Little Miss Perfect—that was the nickname they'd given Brionna. There was something about her that just seemed off. Maybe it was the plastic smile she always gave the cameras, or the way she had a canned answer for any question asked by a reporter. But it was hard not to feel jealous of the gorgeous brunette. Did Brionna know that only a few days before she and Adam had gotten together, he'd been kissing Charlotte?

Probably not. Adam would have kept that information to himself, no doubt.

"Right," Emma deadpanned. "Because hotel managers always vacation on a foreign continent while an important conference is being held at their hotel."

"A girl can dream," Charlotte said. A lock of hair fell into her eyes, and she tucked it behind one ear. The blonde color still surprised her every time she looked in a mirror. She'd needed a change after Adam disappeared and dying her hair had fit the bill. The fact that her natural brown hair color was nearly identical to Brionna's was just a coincidence.

"For your sake, I hope you're right and that he's sitting on some beach in Greece right now," Emma said. She stared out the window and let out a contented sigh. "Not that his view could be any better than this. I had no idea Africa was so beautiful."

That much was true at least. Charlotte stared out the window, trying to push away her negative emotions and just enjoy the moment. In the distance, a long, brown spotted neck reached for leaves high on a tree. Her heart gave a feeble, happy flutter.

That was an actual giraffe in the wild. She was cruising through the African savanna. This was the chance of a lifetime, and she didn't want to spend her entire trip being angry.

"It's like something out of a postcard," Charlotte said. "No wonder the boys always kept the international engagements for themselves."

"And I thought they were just being gentlemanly." Emma smirked. "Think we'll have any time for sightseeing?"

"Maybe. I asked Becky to try to fit a safari ride into the schedule, even if it's only a short one." Her personal secretary was usually able to accommodate those types of requests, and the hotel website advertised safari rides as short as ninety minutes. Charlotte had spent most of the eleven-hour plane ride from Durham researching the Hotel Montgomery. Situated on the edge of tribal lands, the resort catered to tourists eager to go on safari and trophy hunters hoping to bag the Big Five. The money from the hunts helped with conservation efforts, while the meat fed the tribes. Although the resort was relatively new—not quite two years old—it had already made a name for itself as a premier travel destination.

Emma gasped, pointing to a lion sprawled in the shade of a tree only a rock's-throw away. It yawned, and Charlotte could make out each individual tooth in the giant mammal's mouth. She gaped, adrenaline mixing with awe. Could a lion attack a moving car? She wasn't sure how fast they could run.

"I can't believe they get so close to the road," Emma said.

"It's incredible," Charlotte agreed. No wonder Adam had been so eager to go home. At the time, she hadn't been able to imagine why he'd chosen to manage one of the South African hotels over one in their native Durham. Now it was starting to make sense.

"What else does the resort have to offer, aside from safaris?" Emma asked. While Charlotte had researched, Emma had paged through fashion magazines. But Charlotte didn't mind that her cousin had let her do all the work.

"There's an elephant sanctuary on the far end of the reserve. Tourists can pay to help the keeper bathe and feed the animals. You can even ride them."

Emma's eyes widened with glee. "Oh, we have to try to make time for that. I wish we could stay longer than three days. There is no way we'll get to everything before it's time to go home."

"Maybe we can come back on vacation sometime," Charlotte said. Extending their trip wasn't an option— not with Alex's wedding coming up in barely more than a week. Three full days at the Hotel Montgomery was all they'd get, and Charlotte wasn't about to let Adam ruin it for her.

She hoped he was in Greece with Little Miss Perfect. She wanted South Africa all to herself.

Charlotte craned her neck, watching as a hawk glided across the sky. It dove down, snatching some small animal from the grasses of the savanna before rising gracefully once more. She ached to run through those tall grasses—well, maybe grasses less infested by lions. To breathe in the fresh air. To truly enjoy this remarkable corner of the world.

They rounded a bend in the road, passing a copse of trees. The hotel sprang into view, and Charlotte's breath caught in her throat.

"Is that it?" Emma asked, leaning forward.

Charlotte could only nod. Gleaming white marble sparkled underneath the harsh African sun like a jewel in the desert. Calling it a resort was almost insulting. The Hotel Montgomery was an oasis. No wonder it had a waiting list nearly nine months out.

Fountains appeared on either side of the road, their long and narrow jets of water bouncing into the air. Charlotte glanced at Joseph, knowing he'd throw a fit if she rolled down the window to get a better view. The blacktop transitioned into red cobblestones. Neatly trimmed flowers and bushes lined the front of the hotel, while the windows arched high overhead.

"It's so beautiful," Charlotte breathed.

"That's like calling the Sistine Chapel pretty," Emma said. "It's magnificent."

Charlotte had to agree. The caravan of cars slowed, pulling around the wide circular driveway. They came to a stop underneath the portico, right in front of the sliding glass doors.

Joseph got out of the car and was quickly met by Emma's two bodyguards and Karla. Charlotte patiently waited for one of them to open the car door. Another fountain was just a few paces away, jets of water shooting nearly ten feet into the air. A large sign with *Hotel Montgomery* etched into the stone sat just in front of it.

The car door finally opened. A blast of hot, dry air hit Charlotte right in the face, so different from the cool humidity she was used to in Durham. She accepted Joseph's hand and exited the car, barely noting that Karla was already stationed near the sliding glass doors.

"Thank you," Charlotte said, smoothing a hand down the front of her skirt. Bellhops were already unloading luggage from the trunks of the cars under Becky's direction, while the four members of the security detail watched the area with wary eyes.

The glass doors slid open, and a man in an impeccable three-piece gray suit strode forward. He was tall, with long legs and a closely shaved beard that defined a strong jawline. His dark hair was styled off his forehead, and his piercing blue eyes seemed to stare right through her. Charlotte's heart stuttered in her chest before beating again at double-time. He'd always had the uncanny ability to see through her façade to what lay underneath.

"Adam," she breathed, then immediately regretting not calling him *Mr. Montgomery*.

"Princess Charlotte." His smooth voice glided over her like water, making her shiver. She'd always loved the deep timbre of his voice. The way it vibrated against her ear when she laid her head against his chest.

She was frozen to the spot, unable to move. He strode toward her, one hand extended. She accepted it without thinking, letting his hand engulf hers. It was pleasantly cool despite the oppressive heat, the grip firm without being painful. Her entire arm warmed with the contact while her mouth grew dry.

"Welcome to Hotel Montgomery," Adam said, releasing her hand after one last squeeze. "We're so pleased you're here."

Chapter Two

Charlotte's hand tingled, and she could still feel the ghost of Adam's skin against her palm. Running into him while in South Africa had always been a possibility—no, more like an inevitability—but she'd never imagined it would happen five seconds after arriving at his hotel.

She was an idiot for not anticipating this outcome. Of course he'd known she was coming and would greet them at the door. Royalty didn't stay at prestigious hotels unbeknownst to the ones running them, and anyway, her name was probably plastered all over the hotel lobby since she was keynoting the conference.

Did it bother him that she was here?

She hoped it drove him crazy. That he'd stayed up all night worrying about her arrival.

Emma nudged Charlotte with one shoulder. She blinked, trying to collect herself. When had Emma gotten out of the car? Charlotte was suddenly very aware of the oppressive African heat, and the way it made her clothes stick to her body. She probably looked like an abandoned cat, her hair limp and clothes wrinkled.

Her hair! The hair she'd dyed blonde when Adam left. Charlotte clutched the novel in her hands, fighting the urge to smooth back her locks. That would only draw more attention to the change.

Emma cleared her throat and extended a hand toward Adam. "I'm sorry, I didn't catch your name."

Charlotte bit her lip, holding back a grin. Emma knew very well who Adam was—had cheerfully spent hours verbally abusing him after Charlotte had found the photo of Adam and Brionna online.

"My apologies, Princess. It seems I've forgotten my manners." He dropped an air kiss over the top of Emma's wrist, smooth as ever. "I'm Adam Montgomery, the chief operations manager at this hotel."

"Montgomery . . ." Emma pursed her lips as though thinking. "No relation to Thomas Montgomery, Earl of Nottingshire, I suppose?"

"My father, Your Highness."

"Ah. Then we're in good hands here, I'm certain. I was so sorry to hear about the passing of your mother last year."

Charlotte's eyes flew to Adam's, catching the glimpse of pain before it cleared.

"Thank you, Your Highness," Adam said.

He'd only mentioned his mother a few times, but the pain in his voice had been evident each time. Breast cancer. They hadn't caught it until it was too late, and treatments had only prolonged the inevitable. Shortly after the funeral, Adam's father had handed over the South African hotel project—the first property Adam had managed entirely on his own—and he'd thrown himself into the task.

Charlotte swallowed hard, feeling uneasy. Why had she fantasized for even a moment that he would be on a beach in Greece with Little Miss Perfect? He'd probably stay by their side the entire trip, making sure everything went according to plan.

Adam motioned to the sliding glass doors that led inside the building, apparently oblivious to Charlotte's inner turmoil. "If you'll follow me, I can accompany you to your suite and make sure you get settled."

"That would be lovely," Emma said. She wrapped an arm tightly around Charlotte's and propelled her forward, lowering her voice. "Your face is an open book. Don't let him know how much he hurt you."

Adam had said something similar once—that he always knew exactly what Charlotte was feeling just by looking into her eyes. It drove Maggie Staton, the head of public relations at the palace, batty. A good royal should always maintain a poker face, but Charlotte had never mastered that particular skill.

The glass doors slid open, sending a wave of cool air over Charlotte. Karla and one of Emma's bodyguards were already inside, while the two remaining members of the security detail hovered close by.

Just inside the lobby, Charlotte was accosted by a larger-than-life poster of herself. The photograph was from the official palace press packet and showed her natural brown hair color. She winced, ignoring the photo and taking in the lobby. It was completely empty, save a receptionist at the gorgeous dark mahogany check-in desk. Charlotte wasn't surprised. No doubt Joseph had coordinated with hotel security to make sure the area was clear.

Their heels clicked across the white marble floors while crystal chandeliers sent rainbows of light across the room. Sleek black couches were arranged around a fireplace large enough to stand upright in. She'd known from the photographs on the hotel's website that the place would be magnificent, but the pictures hadn't prepared her for the reality. Lord Nottingshire had truly outdone himself with this project, although Charlotte knew Adam had been heavily involved from day one.

"This is quite the hotel you've got here," Emma said, echoing Charlotte's own thoughts.

Adam threw a knee-melting smile over his shoulder. "Thank you. We're extremely proud of Hotel Montgomery. It received five stars in *World Traveler Magazine* last year, and I just confirmed this morning that Natalie and Shawn Erickson will be staying here in October. I'm hoping she gives us a glowing review on *According to Natalie*."

"That is impressive," Charlotte said. Natalie's online travel site had exploded into popularity two years earlier after an article about how she'd fallen in love on a Toujour singles cruise went viral. "I've been following her ever since she visited Durham last year. She's so funny and down-to-earth."

"Yes, and of course she also has connections to Toujour." Another smile from Adam. "I'm hoping to convince them to host one of their singles retreats right here at Hotel Montgomery."

That would be fantastic publicity for the hotel. Charlotte opened her mouth to congratulate him, but caught sight of Emma's raised eyebrow.

What was she doing? Charlotte quickly shut her mouth. Adam was no longer her friend, or more than a friend, or whatever he'd been back in Durham. She couldn't allow herself to fall back into the easy conversation they'd shared then. Opening up had never come easily for Charlotte, but something about Adam made her relax and want to share her secrets.

"Well, that all sounds very exciting," Emma said.

Adam shot Charlotte a glance that she couldn't quite read. "Yes, I'm very happy with how well the hotel has done."

Montgomery Hotels & Resorts had a worldwide reputation for excellence, but this was on a whole other level. She knew how much this success meant to him. How hard he had worked to prove himself to his father, even if he was half a world away most of the time.

"Was there ever any question?" Emma asked, giving a polite laugh that no one but Charlotte would recognize as forced.

"I certainly try my best," Adam said.

They arrived at a set of gleaming gold elevator doors, and Joseph pushed the *up* button while Karla scanned the hallway. Charlotte could feel Adam's eyes on her, but she refused to meet them.

Why, out of all the employees in this hotel, had he decided to be the sole member of their welcoming party? Adam had to know that he was the last person on the planet she wanted to make small talk with. Sure, he was the hotel manager at this property, but wasn't there a public relations specialist better suited to the task?

The elevator doors slid open. Joseph quickly inspected the interior, then motioned them inside. No doubt Karla was checking out the stairwell or something with Emma's guards.

Soft classical music filled the elevator as the doors slid closed. Charlotte clasped her hands tightly together, taking comfort in the weight of the novel in her hands. She was all too aware of Adam's presence—the spicy scent of his aftershave, the fine cut of his suit, the way his blue eyes made her heart throb.

"There's a welcome dinner tonight in the main dining hall at eight o'clock," Adam said. "Most of the conference's special guests are arriving sometime today, and they're all very eager to meet Your Royal Highnesses."

"How lovely," Emma said.

A welcome dinner? Charlotte felt her cheeks heat at the thought of spending even more time with Adam. Her secretary, Becky, hadn't mentioned any welcome dinner.

"We'll have to make sure there is room in our schedules," Charlotte said. This elevator was far too small for her taste. "All of that goes through my secretary."

"Yes, I sent an official invitation to the palace nearly two weeks ago," Adam said. Was that a smirk? "Your secretary accepted it on your behalf."

Charlotte pressed the book closer to her stomach, forcing herself to take slow, even breaths. That was the problem with a secret relationship—your secretary didn't know to refuse invitations that forced you to spend more time with your ex.

The elevator doors slid open, and Charlotte exhaled in relief. She quickly stepped into the hallway, noting Karla and one of Emma's bodyguards were already there.

"I guess I didn't pay too close of attention to our itinerary," Charlotte said. Oh, how she wanted to rail at Adam—to scream that this conference was about bringing education to underdeveloped areas, not drinking cocktails and making small talk. But she knew that socializing was an important part of the next few days, and she would grudgingly play her part.

"A side effect of being a princess," Adam murmured.

Charlotte's spine stiffened at the phrase—one they'd joked about often during those ten days they'd spent together. "I'm rather tired, Mr. Montgomery. Which way to our room?"

"Yes, of course," Adam said, all formality once more. "My apologies, Your Highness. It's the presidential suite at the end of the hallway."

Charlotte waited as Adam unlocked the door and let them inside the suite. Joseph immediately disappeared down one of the hallways, no doubt to do a sweep of the rooms.

The suite was spectacular, with floor-to-ceiling glass doors covering an entire wall and offering a breathtaking view of the savanna. A black baby grand piano sat tucked into one corner of the room, and white couches framed a cozy fireplace, with an animal-skinned rug—a cheetah, perhaps?—in front of it. The sidebar boasted a gorgeous basket of colorful fruit and a dining room table big enough for eight. But Charlotte felt more tightly coiled than a spring, and couldn't appreciate the splendor.

Was Adam still with Brionna? Charlotte assumed they were still together, but she wasn't certain. Little Miss Perfect might be somewhere in the hotel right now.

Charlotte glanced over at Adam. His eyes were on her, face unreadable. She quickly looked away again, focusing on an abstract painting in the dining room. Was it supposed to be a lion? She wasn't sure.

Becky bustled into the room, directing the bellhops with their carts of luggage and breaking some of the tension. Thank heaven. Charlotte sent Emma a pleading expression.

Emma clasped her hands together and smiled broadly. "Well, thank you for your help, Mr. Montgomery. We'll see you tonight at the welcome dinner."

Adam blinked, clearly surprised at the dismissal. Charlotte ignored his questioning stare. He'd closed that door forever, and she wasn't about to humiliate herself by mistaking a casual glance for affection and trying to re-open it.

"I'll see you tonight, then?" Adam asked her. It was a question—one Charlotte wasn't about to give him the satisfaction of answering.

Emma took a step forward, herding Adam toward the door. "Yes, we'll see you tonight."

Adam paused in the doorway, his soulful eyes still trying to pull Charlotte in. "Please let me know if you need anything."

She wanted to throw her book at him. Need anything? She needed him to stop looking at her like there was unfinished business between them. Needed him to leave her alone and assign someone else to be their contact here at the hotel.

"We'll be fine," Charlotte said, her words clipped.

Emma took another step forward, placing one hand on the door. "Goodbye, Mr. Montgomery," she said.

"Goodbye," he echoed.

Emma firmly closed the door, turning to Charlotte.

"Well," she said. "That was incredibly awkward and uncomfortable. So much for avoiding him during the conference."

Charlotte let out a moan, collapsing onto the couch. "How am I going to survive the next three days?"

Emma sat down beside Charlotte, patting her back consolingly. "It'll be fine. I'll run interference tonight, and hopefully Adam will be too busy to bother you during the conference."

"Yes, I suppose you're right," Charlotte said. "There's nothing else to be done. I'll try to ignore him as much as possible."

"Good plan," Emma said. She rose, heading toward the balcony. "I'm going to check out the rest of the suite. Want to come?"

"Sure," Charlotte said, rising as well.

Three days, and then Adam would be out of her life forever. What could possibly go wrong?

Chapter Three

*A*dam couldn't get his encounter with Charlotte out of his head. Lunch found him sitting in the dining room with Brionna, dragging his fork tines through the vinaigrette salad dressing as he remembered the way Charlotte's eyes had flashed when she saw him that morning. The clink of silverware against fine china plates echoed off the fifteen-foot high coffered ceilings, but Adam barely noticed.

He hadn't wanted to be the one to greet her. But no one knew about Adam's fling with the princess of Durham, and it would look insulting to the crown if he passed the task off to anyone else. He was heir to the earldom—a member of the nobility—and Adam didn't want to give his father anything else to criticize. In just a few hours, his father would arrive at the resort, and no doubt he'd have enough complaints without Adam adding wood to the fire.

His mother's death had been hard for all of them, and Adam had been eager to lighten his father's load by taking over the management of the Hotel Montgomery. This hotel was his baby—the first project his father had allowed Adam to take complete charge of. And no princess was going to distract him from seeing it through to completion.

He'd known seeing her again today would be uncomfortable. What Adam hadn't expected was the surge of emotions that had surfaced when he grasped Charlotte's hand.

Would she have lunch delivered to her suite, or would she come down to the dining room?

"Adam? Are you even listening to me?"

He blinked, focusing on Brionna. Her chocolate brown hair was pulled back in a loose bun at the nape of her neck, and she'd left a few strands framing her face. Pale blue eyes stared out at him from peaches-and-cream skin dusted with freckles. She was twenty-nine, same as him, and had a thin frame and delicate features. There wasn't a man alive who would deny that she was pretty.

But Charlotte was so much more than a pretty face. She had a sharp, biting wit that Adam adored. A passion for education and literacy that he admired. A vulnerability that made him want to protect her at all costs.

What Charlotte didn't have was the approval of his deceased mother, or a hotel empire to make his father proud.

Adam had been shocked to return from Durham to find Brionna staying at his hotel. It had felt like his mother was gently prodding him from beyond the grave to finally date the oldest Cartwright heir. Mother had always hoped he and Brionna would eventually end up together.

"Sorry," Adam said. "What were you saying?"

"I said I spoke with Blessing, and she's threatening to quit again." Brionna's brow pinched with worry. "I'm concerned that this time, she might follow through. Last night's vandalism really rattled her."

Adam set down his fork, despite the fact that half of his arugula salad still filled the plate. Blessing was the project coordinator for the school they were building a mile from the resort, and they desperately needed to keep her happy until the project's conclusion. "She's just blowing off steam."

Brionna pursed her lips into a thin line. "Not this time. This is serious, Adam. The council is threatening to sue for breach of contract if we don't open the school by the first of September."

He already knew all of this—not that his father had bothered to give him a heads up before he started managing the Hotel Montgomery. What Adam didn't know was how to fix the problem.

He took a slow sip of his water, giving himself time to think before responding. Adam had known that opening the resort so close to tribal lands, which were protected by strict conservation laws, wouldn't be easy. The deal had nearly fallen through, until the chieftain came up with a compromise—they would sell Montgomery Hotels & Resorts the land, provided the hotel built and funded a school for the tribe's children to attend.

At the time, the compromise had seemed perfect. The school could be run as a charitable nonprofit, which would give the hotel great PR with the locals and help funnel away some money they'd otherwise pay in taxes. Then Adam's mother had been diagnosed with cancer, and he hadn't thought about the school again until arriving in South Africa six months earlier to find the project woefully behind schedule due to push-back from angry members of the tribe. His father had failed to even break ground on the project.

But Adam hadn't let that deter him. He'd immediately set to work getting things back on schedule. And that's when the problems had really started.

Challenges had surfaced almost immediately—little things that chipped away at construction deadlines. The contract had specified the school be opened last September, but his father had begged for leniency due to Mother's rapidly declining health. Now, the tribe's patience was at an end. If they followed through on their threats and sued, Montgomery Hotels & Resorts would probably owe them a hefty settlement for damages, not to mention the goodwill they'd lose from the locals, and the respect Adam would lose from his father.

He couldn't let that happen. Wouldn't let it.

"I'll talk to Blessing tomorrow," Adam said. "I know there have been some setbacks, but we can still open by September if we pick up the pace." No doubt that was exactly what Blessing wanted to hear. Nothing like begging for overtime to make her want to stick around.

"You need new security at the construction site," Brionna said, cutting her salad with a knife. "The guards we have now are clearly being bought off. Either that or they're just atrocious at their job."

"I don't think we need to worry about the security company, but I'll look into it," Adam promised. It took a lot of effort to keep his reply free of snark. Brionna often spoke to him as though he were a child she needed to command, but he knew it was a side effect of her childhood. She'd practically raised her triplet half-brothers alone, despite only being a few years their senior. It was probably partly why Adam's mother had taken Brionna under her wing. The Cartwrights and Montgomerys had seen a lot of each other, since the patriarchs of both families owned hotel empires.

"I hope you do more than look into it," Brionna said. "I've never heard of so much vandalism at a work site. It isn't normal. If my father finds out what's happening here, we'll both be in hot water."

"He won't find out," Adam said.

Brionna was a good woman, Adam reminded himself. A little interfering, perhaps, but she'd make a loyal and dedicated wife. Not that he was anywhere close to proposing. Adam had never so much as held Brionna's hand, and they'd never put a label on their relationship. But he knew that everyone, Brionna included, expected a proposal by the end of the year. It was what his mother would have wanted. He needed to remember that.

"Good. Did I tell you I'm heading to Johannesburg for a few days next week? My father found some more locations for me to check out there."

"Keep me updated," Adam said, even though he didn't really care. It was why Brionna had come to South Africa in the first place—to choose a location for the first ever Cartwright hotel in South Africa.

Adam had eagerly accepted Brionna's invitation to dinner that night after he returned from Durham. The pain of leaving Charlotte had still been fresh in his heart, and the panic of nearly throwing away everything he'd spent a lifetime building fresh in his mind.

He'd been so close to staying in Durham to pursue a relationship with the princess. Which would have been insane. He'd spent more than two decades preparing for a career in hotel management—one his parents had groomed him for. He'd known Charlotte ten days.

So he'd flirted with Brionna at dinner, because his mother would have approved. And they talked hotel business, because his father would expect it. Soon Adam had agreed to let Brionna use the Hotel Montgomery as her home base while she searched for properties. As issues with the school arose, he'd taken advantage of Brionna's listening ear and appreciated her suggestions. Now she was nearly as involved in the school's construction as he was. Sometimes he wondered if that was wise.

"I definitely will," Brionna said. She took another dainty bite of her perfectly cut salad, then looked up at him from beneath lowered lashes. "One of the properties is in a prime location downtown—perfect for a high-rise. Didn't you say that Montgomery was looking to open a location there?"

"Yes," Adam said slowly. "But so is Cartwright."

Brionna lifted her shoulder in a delicate shrug. "Maybe one day we can embark on a project together."

The hints had become more and more obvious over the past six weeks. But that was okay, because Adam was going to propose to Brionna. Eventually. Probably.

It wasn't that she wasn't attractive. It was just that Adam wasn't attracted to her. He'd wished he was more times than he could count, but Brionna was like a sister, or maybe a cousin, that he was especially fond of.

And Charlotte was . . . well, she was indescribable.

Adam hadn't meant to date her while in Durham. The hotel was his life. But he'd seen her across the room at some tediously boring official function and been instantly smitten. She was beautiful in the glossy magazine covers she often graced, but she was gorgeous in person.

He shook off his thoughts. Adam needed to pay attention to Brionna, not daydream about Charlotte. True, there wasn't that intense heat with Brionna that he'd experienced with Charlotte. But Brionna had a solid business head on her shoulders, and the two of them would make an excellent team. His mother had known that, and so did Adam.

Brionna's phone buzzed, and she picked it up from the table. "That's my reminder to get ready for the conference call. Mind if I duck out?"

"Not at all. I think I'm finished eating, too."

"Walk me out, then."

Adam nodded and rose. He rested his hand at the small of Brionna's back, barely touching, and guided her from the dining room. In the hallway she turned, placing a quick kiss on his cheek and giving him a full smile.

Maybe they weren't in love, but they definitely felt a strong affection for each other. That was more than enough to build a lasting relationship. Couples had made it work on less.

"I'll see you at the welcome dinner tonight?" Brionna asked.

"I'll pick you up at seven-thirty," Adam confirmed.

"Make it seven. I want to make sure the staff has everything in order before the guests start to arrive."

That wasn't Brionna's job, but it didn't matter. Adam watched her walk away, swallowing back emotions he couldn't quite define.

Brionna was steady and dependable. She was a ruthless businesswoman, but had a softer side when the occasion called for it, too.

He ran a hand over his jaw as she disappeared around the corner. Charlotte had caught him off guard, that was all.

Adam headed to his office, hoping his assistant was back from the school by now. Keith was indeed already in Adam's office, tapping away at his tablet.

The office was magnificent, with a polished teak wood desk, lush animal prints, and marble floors. But it was all his father's taste, and Adam had never felt comfortable behind the executive desk. Still, he took a seat, not letting his discomfort show.

"How bad is it?" Adam asked.

Keith let out a sigh. He was a few years older than Adam and relatively short, with a balding head and stocky frame. "Well, it could have been worse, which I guess is the good news. The vandals managed to destroy most of the drywall on the main floor before the security guards spooked them. Blessing is furious. The general contractor says we'll have to rip out all the drywall and replace it."

Adam leaned back in his chair with a groan. That would cost a fortune, not to mention the loss of time. "How do they keep getting in there?"

Keith shrugged. "I hate to say it, but maybe Brionna is right, and it's time to question the security guards. Might not be a bad idea to replace them entirely with a new company."

"We've used Edgemont Security for more than a decade at our other South African properties without any issues." Adam didn't know why, but it irked him that Keith was listening to Brionna's advice. "I really don't think they're the problem."

Keith grunted, but didn't argue. "At any rate, Blessing says this will set us back at least another week or two. She's pretty mad."

Adam ran a hand through his hair, frustrated. "I just don't get it. You'd think we were trying to poison the tribe, not educate their children for free."

"I guess change is never easy," Keith said. "I don't understand it, either."

It would be so easy to throw up his hands and call the project off. If people hated the idea of the school that badly, well, that was fine with Adam. He certainly didn't need the added stress and expense of the project.

He'd been ready to cancel the whole thing before going to Durham, whatever promises they'd made in the contract. True, most of the tribe members were eager for the school's opening, but the few who weren't had managed to make Adam's life miserable.

But then he'd met Charlotte. Hearing her speak so passionately about education, and listening to her talk about her desire to one day open her own school, had convinced him to see the project through to its conclusion, whatever the cost. Not finishing the school would disappoint Charlotte. And he couldn't stand that thought, even if they were no longer secretly together.

"How did it go with the princesses?" Keith asked.

Adam blinked, his trance broken. "Fine," he said quickly. Had it been a bit too quick? He'd never told a soul about his relationship with the eldest princess of Durham. Charlotte had wanted to keep the relationship secret, and that had been fine with Adam. "I think they liked the suite. At least, I didn't hear any complaints."

35

Keith gave Adam an odd look. "Why would they have any complaints?"

He'd have to be smoother than this if he didn't want people to get suspicious. "They wouldn't," Adam said. "I just really need this conference to go well. If the delegates from the tribe see we're serious about education, they might be willing to negotiate another extension on the school's opening deadline if it comes to that. I'm not sure how many more setbacks we can handle and still open in September."

"Princess Charlotte is an eloquent speaker and passionate advocate for education," Keith said. "I'm sure everyone in attendance will be inspired by her keynote address. The delegates from the tribe have to see how hard we're working here. Yeah, we're nearly a year behind schedule, but there were extenuating circumstances."

Adam focused on his desk, pretending to rearrange the pens near his keyboard. Extenuating circumstances. That was one way to describe his mother's illness and death. "I'm sure everything will work out in the end. We've made a lot of progress in the last six months."

"Yes, and I think the princesses will be impressed. Are they still planning on attending the welcome dinner tonight?"

Emma was. Adam wasn't sure if Charlotte would be in attendance. She'd seemed pretty angry, but hopefully her sense of duty would be stronger than her fury. "Of course."

"That's good, then. The conference is already off to a great start."

Adam nodded. "I want their comfort to be our top priority during their stay. We'll stick to their sides like glue tonight. Make sure they're introduced to the right people, especially the delegates from the tribe."

"You've got it," Keith said. "Everything will go great, I'm sure."

Adam hoped Keith was right. One thing was for certain—tonight would be very interesting.

Chapter Four

$\mathcal{E}$mma poked her head into Charlotte's bedroom, a smile on her painted lips. "Ready?"

Charlotte turned to the full-length mirror, smoothing down the shimmery champagne-colored gown she'd chosen for the welcome dinner. She'd pulled back the drapes on the large picture windows, and sunlight streamed across the room, making the dress glow. "Do you think this is too flashy?"

Emma pursed her lips, stepping fully into the room. She walked a slow circle around Charlotte, head cocked to one side.

This was why Charlotte had asked Emma's opinion instead of Becky's or Karla's—she always answered honestly.

"No, I don't think so," Emma said at last. "The teardrop pearl earrings help make it more dinner party than black-tie event, and leaving off a necklace was a good choice with the higher neckline. I think you look great."

Emma knew fashion, and she could always be counted on to tell the truth. But still, Charlotte felt uncertain.

"I don't know." Charlotte brushed aside a strand of blonde hair. She'd pulled her loose curls back in a low bun, leaving her neck bare, but had left a few strands to frame her face. Maybe she shouldn't have dyed her hair. She'd always had a pale complexion, and the blonde color seemed to wash it out even more than usual. Or maybe it was just the sunlight pouring through the windows. It seemed brighter here than in Durham. More intense.

Emma folded her arms, raising one eyebrow. She'd chosen a navy blue dress, but had pulled her hair up in a similar fashion to Charlotte's. "Is this about Adam?"

Charlotte's hands stilled, and she dropped them to her sides. "What? Of course not. Don't be ridiculous."

Emma put a hand to her chest, one hip popped. "Oh, I'm being ridiculous? The two of you couldn't stop flirting earlier today. It was nauseating."

"What?" Charlotte grabbed a clutch from her bed and snapped it open, verifying that the essentials were inside—lipstick, hairpins, a small packet of breath mints. "That wasn't flirting. We barely managed to be civil to each other."

"That's exactly what I'm talking about. You're not going to fall under his spell again, are you?"

Charlotte might have snorted, if she did such a thing. "You have nothing to worry about, Emma. I plan to avoid Adam Montgomery as much as possible during our stay. We'll socialize with the government officials and professors at tonight's dinner, then escape the conference whenever possible over the next three days to enjoy some sightseeing. Okay?"

Emma's eyes were unblinking, her expression saying quite clearly that she wasn't convinced. "I just don't want you to get hurt again."

Charlotte tucked her clutch under one arm and slipped into her high heels. "The only person who's going to get hurt is Adam if he tries to mess with me. I'll sic Joseph on him. It's been a while since he's had a good take-down."

Emma laughed. "He has been looking a little dour lately."

"See? Everything will be fine." Charlotte gave herself one last cursory glance in the mirror. "Let's go."

Their security details waited in the living room, their black suits pressed and expressions alert.

"Think we can escape by eleven o'clock tonight?" Emma asked as she grabbed her clutch from the coffee table. She hid a yawn. "I'm already exhausted."

"Sure." Charlotte smirked. "I bet Joseph here will let us take a nice run without our security detail, too."

"Not on your life, Your Highness," Joseph said, his tone stern.

Emma laughed, tapping Joseph's chest with her clutch. "You're no fun."

"And there's no way this party is going to end before midnight," Charlotte said.

Becky breezed into the room then, her hair falling gently around her shoulders and a conservative green dress swishing about her legs.

"I doubt we'll be back before one o'clock," she said, glancing at the tablet that seemed permanently affixed to her arm. "There will be quite a few people in attendance tonight, including the Earl of Nottingshire."

"Adam's father?" Charlotte asked in surprise.

Becky nodded. "Yes, he just arrived at the hotel an hour ago. I believe he flew in from Thailand."

A knock echoed through the room, interrupting the conversation.

Charlotte turned to Emma. "Are you expecting someone?"

"No," Emma said, her eyes wide. "You?"

"No," Charlotte said slowly.

Adam wouldn't show up to escort them to dinner, would he?

"That will be Mr. Montgomery," Becky said, motioning for Karla to get the door. "Princesses never enter an official function without an escort."

Emma put a hand to her mouth, her shoulders shaking with suppressed giggles while Charlotte glared. It hadn't been easy keeping her relationship with Adam from Becky, but she wasn't about to let the cat out of the bag now. Luckily, Becky's back was turned, and she didn't see Emma laughing.

"I'm sure that Mr. Montgomery has much more pressing matters to attend to than walking us to dinner," Charlotte said, holding her clutch close to her chest. She wished she dared fit a book in it, even though it would be extremely rude to read at the dinner—not that she'd have time, anyway. Just a small volume, perhaps one of Shakespeare's plays.

"Nonsense," Becky said. "You are his top priority for the next three days, I'm certain."

Charlotte seriously doubted that. He probably couldn't wait for her to head back to Durham, so he could return to his fairytale existence with Little Miss Perfect.

Karla rested a hand on her gun and peered through the peephole, then opened the door.

"Good evening," said Adam's smooth voice. "I'm here to escort Their Royal Highnesses Princess Charlotte and Princess Emma to dinner."

Karla stepped aside, holding the door. "Come in."

"Thank you."

Charlotte put a hand to her throat, her breath catching at the sight of Adam. He'd changed from his gray suit to a black tuxedo with a blue silk vest and tie that brought out the color of his eyes. His wavy hair shone underneath the chandelier light, and it looked like he'd trimmed his beard.

Charlotte tightened her grip on her clutch, stomach quivering. She'd always had a love-hate relationship with that beard. Loved the way it felt against her skin when they kissed. Hated how hard it made it to hide the evidence of their time together. Curse her sensitive skin that always turned red after a few hours spent kissing him.

Emma leaned close, her voice low enough that only Charlotte could hear. "If you're trying to keep what happened in Durham a secret, you're doing a horrible job of it right now."

Charlotte flinched, trying to school her expression. Adam's eyes were still on her, no doubt taking in every emotion that had flickered across her face. Fantastic.

"Good evening, Mr. Montgomery," Charlotte said. Could Becky hear the tremble in her voice? "Thank you for accompanying us tonight."

"My pleasure," Adam said. "Are you ready to go?"

Charlotte glanced at Emma, who nodded in confirmation.

"Yes, we're ready," Emma said.

Adam nodded and held out an arm to both of them. "Let's go then."

Slowly, Charlotte slipped her arm into the crook of Adam's elbow, remembering the first time he'd offered it—at the charity event where they'd met. Heat sparked at the touch, spreading up her arm and to her neck.

So stupid. This touch meant less than nothing to him.

She let him lead her, along with Emma, from the room, holding onto his arm with only the tips of her fingers and keeping as much distance between them as possible. The door clicked shut behind them, and the small entourage headed toward the elevators.

Adam pulled Charlotte close, his warm breath caressing her ear as he whispered, "I know I'm the last person on earth you want to spend time with, but you could at least try to hide your distaste."

Charlotte flinched, glancing over her shoulder. Becky was a few paces behind them, a cell phone pressed to her ear. Good.

"I don't know what you're talking about," Charlotte said.

"Stop being coy. Your face has always been an open book."

"Well, pardon me for having feelings," Charlotte snapped. "Let's just survive these next three days, and then we never have to speak to each other again."

The elevator dinged open then, and the close confines of the room prevented further conversation on the matter.

In the ballroom, the party was already in full swing, just as Charlotte had known it would be. Becky would never allow them to arrive before things were up and running. It just wasn't done.

"Introducing Her Royal Highness Princess Charlotte of Durham, and Her Royal Highness Princess Emma of Durham," a voice echoed across the loudspeaker.

Charlotte immediately dropped her arm from Adam's and took a step away from him. Polite clapping filled the room, and she nodded in what she hoped was a regal fashion to those present.

Music filled the room once more, and the guests soon returned to their original conversations, which was just the way Charlotte liked these introductions to go. The ballroom was gorgeous, with fifteen-foot-high coffered ceilings and three elegant chandeliers. Large arched windows looked out over the savanna, where a blood-orange sun disappeared behind the horizon. Her security detail disappeared into the crowd, as they were prone to do at these events, while Becky stayed nearby in case Charlotte needed her.

A waiter passed by, and Adam grabbed two champagne glasses, handing one to Charlotte and the other to Emma before grabbing one for himself. "Most of the people here tonight are professors from universities around the country, but we also have members of the national education board in attendance and a few delegates from the local tribe."

"The tribe?" Emma asked, her brow furrowed in confusion.

Adam nodded. "The Hotel Montgomery is building a school about a mile from here. Any child who lives on the wildlife preserve can attend for free."

"Ah." Emma nodded, her eyes lightening. "I think Charlotte mentioned something about that."

Charlotte felt her cheeks grow red and quickly took a sip of her champagne. Adam had told her all about the school while in Durham, and she'd confided to Emma how jealous she was that he was getting to live out her dream. She'd been advocating for education and literacy for years, yet all of her attempts to start a private school for inner-city children in Castlebridge had been thwarted. *That's why we have public schools,*" her mother always said when Charlotte brought up the subject. *"I refuse to allocate our funds to something that taxpayer money already pays for. Keep focusing on improving the schools we already have."*

Maybe her mother had a point, but that didn't stop Charlotte from dreaming.

A stocky man appeared then, with a balding head and kind eyes.

"Allow me to introduce you to my assistant, Keith," Adam said, motioning to the man.

"Your Highnesses," Keith said, shaking their hands. "Such an honor."

"It's nice to meet you as well," Charlotte said. Odd—she felt like she knew Keith, even though they'd never met. Adam had often talked about how invaluable the man's help had been since he took over management of the resort.

"Please, let me know if you need anything during your stay," Keith said. Then he turned his attention to Adam. "Blessing is here."

Adam's shoulders sagged with relief, and he nodded. "Thank you. We'll go and find her now."

Keith nodded and walked away.

"Who's Blessing?" Emma asked.

"The project manager of our school," Adam said.

More like the woman he worried was cracking under the stress. Charlotte had heard a lot about Blessing, too. How she was very qualified for the position, but frustrated by the constant delays they kept experiencing. But Adam said there wasn't time to bring someone else up to speed and still open the school by September, so he tried to keep Blessing happy as much as possible.

"Ah, there she is," Adam said. His face suddenly transformed, and he walked to where a woman stood along one wall. She was short, with dark hair and wide-set eyes. Based on the fine lines just beginning to form around her mouth, Charlotte would guess the woman was somewhere in her early fifties.

"Mr. Montgomery," Blessing said, setting her champagne glass on the side-table she stood beside. Her eyes flicked to Charlotte and Emma, then back to Adam.

"Good to see you," Adam said, giving her a quick handshake. "Blessing, may I introduce you to Their Royal Highnesses Princess Charlotte and Princess Emma of Durham."

Blessing let out a nervous laugh, then quickly dropped into a clumsy curtsy. "Your Highnesses, it is such an honor."

Charlotte instantly slipped into her princess persona, taking Blessing's hand in hers and giving it a squeeze. "The pleasure is entirely ours," she said. "I've heard so much about the School Montgomery and the work you're doing there."

Blessing put a fluttery hand to her chest. "It's been quite the undertaking. You've been such an inspiration to us as we work on the project, Princess Charlotte."

Now Charlotte was the one feeling uncomfortable. "That means a lot to me. Education is something I feel very passionately about, and I love what you're trying to do with the school. I do hope I can see it before heading back to Durham."

"There's a tour tomorrow morning," Blessing said quickly.

Charlotte nodded. "I'll see to it that my secretary puts it on my schedule."

"Already done, Your Highness," Becky said.

"Excellent," Charlotte said. "I'm looking forward to it."

They exchanged pleasantries with Blessing for a few more minutes. She was a nervous woman, with her eyes constantly darting about and her hands never still. But her passion for education was clear, and Charlotte could see why Adam had hired her.

As for Adam, he was a perfect host, introducing them to all the right people and seamlessly ending conversations before they dragged on too long. Charlotte had forgotten just how charismatic he was. How people seemed drawn to him. She certainly had been.

The introductions went on eternally, with Becky whispering any useful tidbits of information in Charlotte's ear while Adam held the attention of whoever they spoke with so no one would notice. Charlotte fought the urge to shift her weight to soothe the aching in her feet. It had to be close to eight o'clock by now. Surely dinner would be served soon.

Across the room, a tall woman lifted her hand in a wave. Adam gave a nod of acknowledgment, then turned his attention back to the man they were speaking with—a local professor of child development.

Charlotte smiled at the man, darting glances across the room whenever Adam's attention was diverted to size up the woman who had waved. The professor had been going on about his gout for what felt like an eternity, and for the first time all night Adam was struggling to end the conversation tactfully.

The woman had long brown hair, a trim figure, and a pretty smile. Brionna. Even across the room, Charlotte knew that it had to be her.

So she was in South Africa with Adam, as Charlotte had suspected. That probably meant they were still together.

Brionna headed toward them. The closer she got, the more certain Charlotte grew of her identity.

"Oh, there's Brionna," Adam said when the professor paused for air. It didn't escape Charlotte's notice that he hadn't prefaced that with *my girlfriend*. Did that mean he and Brionna weren't together? "Thanks so much for joining us at the conference. We'll talk more later."

"Of course," the professor said, offering a quick head nod. "So excellent to speak with you, Your Highnesses. I look forward to your keynote on Friday evening."

"Thank you," Charlotte said.

The man left, and Brionna walked over with a broad smile on her face.

"Your Highnesses," she said, extending a hand. "It is such a pleasure to meet you both."

Charlotte accepted the outstretched hand, too stunned to ignore it. Brionna's grip was firm and assured—a handshake usually only given by businessmen. She hadn't waited for an introduction, just boldly said hello.

"This is Brionna Cartwright," Adam said.

Why did he keep leaving off a relationship status when introducing her? It was infuriating. Charlotte knew she shouldn't care, but she was dying to know if he and Brionna were still together.

Maybe they never had been a couple. The internet lied all the time—she knew that much from Alex's experiences. But then why hadn't Adam ever called her?

"Charmed," Emma said in an overly sweet tone. Charlotte hid a smile. It was Emma's *kill them with kindness* voice, not that anyone else would recognize it. "What brings you to the Hotel Montgomery, Miss Cartwright? I thought I'd read somewhere that you were managing properties in Germany at the moment."

"No," Brionna said brightly. She obviously hadn't heard the danger behind Emma's tone. "I've actually been in South Africa for—oh, what's it been now, Adam? Six weeks?"

Adam's eyes flicked to Charlotte's, then away again. "About that."

"I'm scouting out locations for a Cartwright hotel," Brionna explained. "Well, that and helping Adam with the school whenever possible. When he told me you'd be keynoting at the conference, Your Highness, I was beyond thrilled. I've been studying your theories on education extensively and find them fascinating. Is it true you hope to open a privately funded school in Durham for children with especially difficult circumstances?"

Charlotte glanced at Adam, wondering if he'd told Brionna this. But her desire to open a school wasn't exactly a secret. No doubt it had come up in some article somewhere.

"Perhaps one day," Charlotte said lightly. "For now, I'm just happy to be at this conference."

"And we're happy to have you," Brionna said. She put a hand on Adam's arm, giving the women a winning smile. "Would you mind terribly if I borrow Adam for just a moment? There's something I need to discuss with him of a time-sensitive nature."

"Of course not," Charlotte lied. It was probably just something about the school. But why was Brionna helping Adam with that project, anyway? Charlotte didn't know much about the Cartwrights—just that they were an American family who ran a hotel empire—but she was pretty sure Brionna didn't know anything about running a school.

"We'll go grab a glass of water," Emma said. She wrapped her arm through Charlotte's. "I'm parched."

"I won't be long," Adam said. "If I don't introduce you to my father soon, he'll have my head."

The words were joking, but Charlotte knew there was probably truth to the statement. That was something else Adam had talked about during their time together—how hard it was to please his father.

Emma led Charlotte toward the water table, smiling at the people they passed.

"I can't believe her," Charlotte hissed. "Who does she think she is?"

Emma lifted one eyebrow. "I thought you'd be glad for the reprieve from Adam."

"Of course I am," Charlotte said. "But something about Brionna just rubs me wrong. She acts like she owns the world or something."

Emma accepted a glass of water from the bartender, and Charlotte did the same.

"So Little Miss Perfect has a flaw," Emma murmured. "Big surprise. You don't still have feelings for Adam, do you? Because I could swear that someone's green with jealousy."

"Don't be ridiculous." Charlotte took a long sip of her water, eying Adam and Brionna. They stood just outside the doors of the ballroom, heads close together as Brionna's arms waved about. She must be one of those people who couldn't talk without her hands. Annoying.

"Char, I know he's smooth," Emma said. "But remember how much he hurt you last time? You don't want to go through that again."

"You're preaching to the choir." Now Brionna's face was tight, her lips pinched together, and Adam had a furrow between his brow. A lover's spat, perhaps?

Emma seemed to notice the same thing. "Trouble in paradise?"

Charlotte swatted her cousin's arm, but couldn't help grinning. "Maybe."

Adam and Brionna headed back into the ballroom then, and Emma set her martini glass of water on the bar counter. "Looks like they're done fighting."

"Time to socialize again," Charlotte agreed with a groan.

Adam approached, offered them a tight smile. "Sorry about that. Are you ready to meet my father?"

"Of course," Charlotte said, setting down her water glass as well.

But the argument between Adam and Brionna wouldn't leave her mind.

Chapter Five

Charlotte knew immediately which man must be Adam's father. He stood around a side-table with two other men, a glass of red wine in one hand and an expression like he'd just sucked a lemon on his face. Lord Nottingshire had the same thick hair as his son, although his was graying at the temples. His eyes were the same blue shade as well, with that trademark Montgomery jawline. The major difference between the two men was that Lord Nottingshire was clean shaven.

Lord Nottingshire must have seen them approaching, because he said something to the men and strode toward them.

"Father," Adam said. "I'd like to introduce you to Their Royal Highnesses, Princess Charlotte and Princess Emma of Durham. Your Highnesses, this is my father, Thomas Montgomery, the Earl of Nottingshire."

"I thought you'd never bring them over," Lord Nottingshire said. His handshake was firm and businesslike, and Charlotte barely held back a wince. "It is such a pleasure to meet Your Highnesses. Of course I've spoken at length with your father at the House of Lords. Gone the rounds with him on a few of the taxes he's suggested for businesses."

Charlotte gave a polite chuckle. "It's nice to finally meet you, Lord Nottingshire. We were so sorry to hear of Lady Nottingshire's passing."

A shadow passed across Lord Nottingshire's face, and he cleared his throat. "Thank you."

"Your hotel is beautiful," Emma cut in, expertly changing the subject. Charlotte was once again grateful her cousin had decided to come on this trip. "Charlotte and I can't get over how sunny it is here."

"Quite a change from Durham," Lord Nottingshire said with a dark chuckle.

"They both have their own kind of beauty," Brionna cut in. "The first time I visited Castlebridge, I was amazed at how green everything was."

So Brionna was defending Durham now. Charlotte gritted her teeth, then jumped when something squeezed her arm. She glanced over at Emma, who gave a sharp shake of her head.

Right. Charlotte's feelings must be written across her face yet again.

A loud, hacking cough ripped through the room, the sound close enough to make Charlotte jump.

Apparently she wasn't the only one. A server with a full tray of champagne glasses stumbled backward, right into Charlotte.

Charlotte thrust out her arms to keep the slight woman from knocking her over just as another cough echoed through the room. At Charlotte's touch, the waitress whirled, tray in hand.

And dumped the champagne all over Charlotte's dress.

Charlotte jumped back with a gasp, feeling the sticky liquid soak through the fabric. Champagne flutes crashed to the floor, and Charlotte jumped again as tiny shards of glass bounced about her ankles.

Karla was at her side in an instant. "Your Highness, are you okay?"

"I'm fine," Charlotte said, pulling her dress away from where it now clung to her legs. There had to have been fifteen glasses of champagne on that tray.

"Char," Adam said, wrapping a hand around her arm. His eyes were dark with concern, and a furrow had formed between his brows. "Are you hurt?"

"I don't think so." Charlotte shook out her hands, sending drops of champagne to the floor. She blinked, trying to clear her head.

"Let's move away from all this glass," Karla said. "Step carefully so you don't get cut."

Charlotte lifted her skirts and obediently stepped away from the mess. The marble floor was slick from the alcohol, and she felt a sting near one ankle where she figured glass had nicked her skin. She craned her neck, looking for the server girl who'd plowed into her. "Is the waitress okay?"

"Brionna's checking on her," Adam said. "Careful, don't slip."

"I really am okay." For the first time, Charlotte realized just how many eyes were on her. At least a dozen people had witnessed the catastrophe and were ogling her. She probably looked like a drowned rat. Fantastic. She lifted a hand in a small wave. "These things happen. No harm done."

The onlookers seemed satisfied with that and returned to their conversations. Good. No sense making a big deal out of a small accident.

"Adam," Lord Nottingshire said tightly. "A word?"

Adam nodded and headed over to his father, while Charlotte picked her way to where the waitress stood with her mouth open wide, eyes brimming with tears. Brionna had an arm wrapped around the girl's shoulder, but she didn't seem to notice.

"Your Highness," the waitress stammered. "I'm so sorry, I didn't—"

Charlotte placed a gentle hand on the girl's arm. She couldn't be more than eighteen, with a pixie nose and tightly coiled curls held back from her face with a headband. Her white server's shirt was splattered with champagne. "It was an accident. Are you hurt?"

The girl reached up, quickly wiping away a tear that had escaped down her cheek. "No. Are you?"

"No," Charlotte said. "That cough startled me too."

"I'll go get someone to clean this up so no one else falls," Brionna said, giving the girl a kind smile before walking away.

Emma took a sip of her own champagne and smiled at the waitress. "This is the most fun I've had at one of these events for a while. Thanks for livening it up."

The woman's dark skin turned pale, and she flicked a glance to where Adam and his father held a hushed conversation. "My apologies again, Your Highness."

It seemed whatever Lord Nottingshire had to say, he was done talking. He strode over to them, his expression dark.

"Do you have any idea what you've done?" he hissed to the waitress. He turned his attention to Charlotte. "I am so sorry, Your Highness. I assure you, this won't happen again."

The waitress took a step back, her eyes wide and afraid. "I'll go get a mop and clean this up immediately, Lord Nottingshire."

"You'll do nothing of the sort," Lord Nottingshire said, his voice clipped. "You're fired."

Charlotte's mouth dropped open, and she could see the surprise and shock in Emma's eyes as well. Fired? It had been an accident.

"I don't think—" Charlotte began.

"Father," Adam cut in, his expression dark. "I hardly think that's necessar—"

"She dumped an entire tray of champagne on a princess," Lord Nottingshire hissed.

"And it wasn't done intentionally," Charlotte broke in. "Please, don't do this."

The waitress lowered her head, brushing once more at her cheeks. She was crying. A lump rose in Charlotte's throat at the sight of the woman's distress.

She wouldn't let her get fired over this. No way.

But before she could say another word, Adam had started speaking again.

"Karabo, why don't you take the rest of the night off," Adam said, giving the waitress a kind smile. "I'll see you tomorrow night for your shift in the dining room."

Karabo's shoulders sagged with relief, and she nodded.

"Please accept my sorrow," she said, bowing low to Charlotte. Then she hurried away.

Adam wasn't going to let the girl get fired. Charlotte glanced over at the murderous expression on Lord Nottingshire's face. And from the looks of it, Adam would pay dearly for his insubordination.

"I really am fine, Lord Nottingshire," Charlotte said, doing her best to give him a pleasant smile. "Please don't fire the girl on my account. In fact, I'll take it as a personal insult if you do."

"Karabo is one of our best employees," Adam said, shooting Charlotte a grateful look. "She's never late and always willing to pick up an extra shift on short notice."

"Well, it seems that's settled then." Emma inclined her head toward the door. "We really should go back to the room so you can change, Char. I expect dinner will be served any minute now."

"I'll hurry then." Charlotte purposefully walked between Adam and his father, wanting them both to take a deep breath and a big step backward. She rested her hand briefly on Adam's hand, mouthing *thank you*.

He gave her hand a squeeze, and Charlotte hurried from the room. But for the rest of the evening, she couldn't forget that moment—the one where Adam defended a scared employee and saved her job. The moment where he reminded Charlotte that he wasn't just good looks and a charismatic personality.

He was also human.

She'd almost forgotten that somewhere inside Adam lay the heart of a gentleman. Charlotte had been so hurt by his abandonment that she'd vilified him, conveniently ignoring all his good traits.

But tonight she'd been reminded just how kind Adam was. And Charlotte wasn't sure she could ever forget again.

Chapter Six

Adam had survived the evening. Could he call it surviving if he felt like he'd been run over by a truck?

He let his shoulders slump as the last of the guests left the ballroom. The soft piano music that had filled the space all evening was replaced by chattering employees and the clink of plates as they cleared the tables.

When Karabo had dumped champagne on Charlotte, Adam had really thought a major blowup was imminent. Not from Charlotte, of course. She'd been gracious and kind about the incident—a true princess. But Adam had seen the fury dancing across his father's face.

It had taken everything in Adam to stand up to his father and prevent Karabo's firing. But he was responsible for the employees at the Hotel Montgomery, and Karabo was one of the best they had. She didn't deserve to lose her job. Not over an honest accident.

Adam headed toward one of the round dinner tables that had already been cleared and grabbed the tablecloth from it, wadding it into a ball. He needed to keep busy, or worry would consume him. Worry about the conference, the school, his father.

Charlotte.

A soft hand landed on Adam's arm, startling him from his thoughts. He glanced at the hand, immediately recognizing the trimmed nails—freshly manicured, of course—and slender fingers. Heat spread up Adam's arm as the subtle scent of vanilla made his head swirl.

Adam turned, looking down at Charlotte. Even in heels, the top of her head barely reached his chin.

She dropped her hand from his arm, taking a step back. After the champagne incident, she'd changed into a deep purple dress with a low back. This fabric didn't shimmer like the other dress had, but it hugged her curves in a way that had Adam's mouth growing dry.

"Hey," he said. "I thought you'd already left."

"Not quite," Charlotte said. "Great job tonight. Seems like there's going to be an excellent turnout tomorrow for the first day of the conference. I was going to try to sneak away with Emma to do some sightseeing, but after talking to some of the professors tonight I really want to attend their presentations."

Adam swallowed, trying to focus on Charlotte's words and not the way her lips looked forming them. The lipstick she'd chosen for tonight was a deep red, darker than anything he'd seen her wear before. He liked it way too much.

"That means a lot, coming from you," Adam said. "I know you've been to a lot of these conferences."

"Nothing put on by Education Beyond Borders, although I've always wanted to. They must have really liked your hotel to choose to hold it here."

"I was very persuasive," Adam said. He relaxed against the edge of the table, the familiarity he always felt with Charlotte washing over him like warm water. "To be honest, I think we'll end up losing money hosting this. But I'm really hoping that this weekend will show the tribe just how serious we are about education."

"Things haven't improved on that front?"

Adam shook his head. "Unfortunately not."

"They'll come around." There was a confidence in her voice that Adam envied. "You're doing a good thing here, Adam."

"I'm not sure my father's motives were entirely altruistic when he signed that deal."

Charlotte lifted her shoulder in a shrug. "Either way, the end result is the same, right? The school is what really matters here."

"Right." Adam shoved his hands in his pockets so he wouldn't try to hold one of hers. "I don't think I ever thanked you for keynoting at the conference. It really means a lot to me."

A shadow passed across her face, and she glanced at the floor. "I didn't do it for you."

Adam blinked. "That's not what I meant—"

"As a princess of Durham, I have a responsibility to use my platform for good. Education Beyond Borders is an excellent organization, and I'm honored to speak at their conference."

"Of course." Adam ran a hand over his jaw. "Sorry again about the champagne earlier. Karabo really is a very good waitress most of the time."

Charlotte's expression darkened, and she tightened her grip on the small purse she carried. Adam wondered if she was hiding a book inside. His mouth twitched, and he pretended to scratch his nose to hide it.

He'd caught Charlotte reading a worn copy of *The Great Gatsby* at the charity ball where they'd met. She'd been nestled in a hidden alcove, leaning against the wall while a potted plant nearly obscured her from view, completely absorbed by the book. That was when he'd known she was someone he wanted to get to know better.

68

"I really thought your father was going to fire that poor girl," Charlotte said.

Karabo. Right.

"She was clearly terrified," Charlotte continued, her voice becoming higher as emotion made her cheeks flush a pretty pink. "I mean, honestly. How was she to know someone would cough loud enough to be heard all the way in Durham? It sounded like a freight train was barreling right through the ballroom."

Adam's mouth twitched, and he longed to pull Charlotte to him in a fierce hug. She'd always had a way with words. It was one of the things he found most attractive about her.

"I'll talk to Karabo tomorrow," Adam assured her. "Let her know that her job isn't threatened."

"But it would have been, if the choice was your father's."

Adam couldn't lie to Charlotte. He pushed back the shame that bubbled up at his father's actions and reminded himself that he was still hurting. Adam's mother hadn't even been gone a year, and his father was handling it the only way he knew how—by becoming a bigger bully than ever.

"Don't worry about Karabo," Adam said. "My father was just upset on your behalf."

"Charlotte," a sharp voice said. Emma strode across the room, her lips pursed into a thin line. "Shouldn't we be getting back to our suite?"

Adam barely held back a sigh. When he'd received an email from the palace saying both princesses would be coming, he hadn't exactly been thrilled. Emma had known about his and Charlotte's relationship, which meant she knew about the breakup, too—and probably was none too pleased with the way he'd handled it. The last thing he needed during this conference were two princesses upset with him.

"Good to see you, Princess Emma," Adam said with a nod. "Did you have a good evening?"

"Simply lovely," Emma said, not giving him so much as a glance. "Ready to go?"

"Ready," Charlotte said, going to her cousin's side before glancing back at Adam. "See you tomorrow for the tour of the school?"

"See you then," Adam agreed.

Charlotte nodded and walked away, Emma right beside her. The two women bent their heads close together, whispering earnestly. Probably talking about him. Adam scratched the back of his neck, wondering what Charlotte had told Emma. They probably both hated him after how he'd behaved.

A strong hand landed on his shoulder and squeezed. "Meet me in my office in five minutes," Adam's father said.

"I will," Adam said.

Except it wasn't Father's office anymore. It was Adam's.

Father gave Adam's shoulder another squeeze, then walked away. Just great. Getting yelled at by his father would be the perfect end to this evening.

Adam found Keith sitting at the bar, his tablet on the counter before him and a glass of scotch nearby.

"Hey," Keith said, glancing up from his tablet. "Want a drink?"

"No, I have a meeting with my father in just a moment," Adam said.

Keith nodded, taking a sip of his scotch. "I think tonight went pretty well other than the champagne incident. Everyone I spoke to seemed very excited for tomorrow's classes. Princess Charlotte was a big hit."

"She always is," Adam said. "Did you get a chance to speak with the delegates from the tribe before they left? I was hoping to say goodbye."

"No, they kind of disappeared," Keith said. "But everything seemed fine when I spoke to them last. They said they'd be there for the tour of the school in the morning."

Adam nodded. "Okay, just thought I'd check."

"Sorry."

"Not your fault. Can you see that everything is cleaned up in here? I'm not sure how long the meeting with my father will take."

"Sure thing, boss." Keith gave a salute. "See you in the morning."

"See you," Adam agreed.

He wished he could stay and oversee the rest of the cleanup. That would be far preferable to a discussion with his father.

Father sat behind Adam's solid teak wood desk. The blueprints for the school were spread across it, and he was hunched over them, studying. His reading glasses had slid to the end of his nose, and a scowl made his face look pinched. Adam honestly couldn't remember the last time he'd seen his father smile. Before Mother's cancer diagnosis, perhaps?

"Sit down," his father commanded, not bothering to look up from the blueprints.

Silence stretched between them. The tick of the second hand on the clock behind Adam's desk echoed loudly, each second seeming to last a minute. Adam had personally commissioned that clock's design from the trunk of a marula tree that had been struck by lightning. He'd given it to his father the day the resort opened, never imagining that one day this office would be his.

Father pulled his glasses off with a sigh, finally giving Adam his attention. "I see you've made some changes to my blueprints."

Adam swallowed, willing himself not to fidget. "Just minor ones."

"You've added an extra set of ovens in the cafeteria."

"After speaking with Blessing, it seemed necessary. I wasn't sure we could efficiently feed two hundred students a day without them."

Father massaged his brow, looking pained. "We didn't promise to feed the students in a certain time frame. Appliances aren't cheap, and I want this project to come in under budget."

"It will," Adam said. He'd make sure of it.

His father nodded, pushing the plans aside and leaning back in his chair. "Tonight was a disaster. I expected better of you, Adam."

The words cut like a knife, but Adam didn't let his hurt show. "I really don't think Princess Charlotte is upset about what happened. How was anyone supposed to know he was going to cough so loudly? I think I jumped a bit myself when it happened."

"That's not the point." His father put a fist to his mouth, his eyes narrowing. "I left you in charge of things here because I thought you could handle it. But after speaking with Blessing tonight, I discovered that things are worse than I realized with the school."

Most of which wasn't Adam's fault. "I'm on top of it."

"You'd better be, because we cannot afford to get sued right now. Finish the school by September first, get another extension from the tribe, renegotiate the terms of the contract—I don't care how you fix things, I just want it done."

Adam wanted to scream at his father. Didn't it matter that most of the problems Adam encountered were a direct result of how his father had handled things when he was in charge?

But he couldn't say that. Would never hurt his father that deeply. He'd only let so many issues crop up because he'd been busy worrying over his wife's ever-failing health. Adam had let his work slide during those three years when Mother was undergoing cancer treatments, too.

Father placed a hand on the desk and leaned forward. "Tonight, a member of the royal family was humiliated."

"I don't think—"

"You challenged my authority in front of an employee," his father continued. "Blessing opened my eyes to just how serious the situation is with the school. And then Brionna told me that it has once again been vandalized."

Brionna had gone behind Adam's back and talked to his father? Adam clenched his jaw, anger flaring. True, Brionna didn't know how badly his relationship with his father had deteriorated in the nine months since his mother's death. It wasn't something they ever talked about. But wasn't there some unwritten rule that you never got parents involved in their adult children's problems?

"Yes, the school was vandalized again." Adam gripped the armrests of his chair, telling himself not to make a scene. "But within hours, we'd assessed the damage and created a plan to fix it. You trusted me to handle this project, Father. So let me handle it."

Father stared at Adam, his eyes unblinking. Finally he nodded and rose, pulling his suit coat from the back of the chair. "You're right, son."

Adam rose as well. "Are you heading to bed?"

"No, to Hong Kong. A car is waiting to take me to the jet."

So he wasn't staying for the conference. Adam didn't know whether to be relieved or disappointed. "I understand. Travel safely."

Father nodded. "Sorry I can't stick around."

"I understand. Can I walk you out?"

Father nodded again.

The front lobby was quiet, the lights dimmed for the evening and the usual soft jazz music turned off. Outside, the air had cooled to a pleasant temperature. Crickets chirped, and the moon was a sliver of light in the distance.

Father paused, one hand on the car door. "Take care of yourself, son."

Adam clasped his hands tightly in front of him. "You too, sir."

"Brionna is a smart girl, with a good head on her shoulders." Father climbed into the car, leaving the door open. "You should listen to her about the security company. Don't let that girl get away."

Adam coughed, shock overcoming him. "Excuse me?"

"You heard me. I'm counting on you, Adam. Don't disappoint me."

Father shut the door, and the car pulled away. Adam stood, watching as the taillights disappeared into the inky darkness of the savanna.

Don't disappoint me. What had his father been referring to—the school? The conference? Adam's undefined relationship with Brionna?

The sliding glass door swooshed open, and Adam walked back inside. Surely his father didn't mean Brionna. Mother had always hinted that they'd make a good couple, but Father had never voiced an opinion one way or the other on Adam's love life.

As Adam crawled into bed that night, his mind still obsessed over all the possible meanings behind that cryptic phrase. His last thought before finally falling asleep was why, after all the times his father had disappointed Adam, he even cared.

Chapter Seven

Charlotte stepped out of the car, glancing up at the school with admiration. It was clearly a homage to nineteenth-century buildings in Durham, with a red brick façade, lots of windows, and a chimney on either side of the roof. She could almost picture ivy cascading down the front of the building, although she doubted it would ever happen. Did ivy grow in the arid South African climate?

Emma emerged behind Charlotte and gave the school an appraising look. "It's got potential," she said finally.

"You just like the Durham design."

"It's a point in Adam's favor," Emma agreed. She took a careful step, eying the ground disdainfully. "Although I hope they're planning on pouring a parking lot at some point."

"It's still a work in progress," Charlotte said. The drywall remnants, bent nails, and the other garbage typical of a construction site were absent—another point for Adam. But the soft dirt was a bit uneven, and Karla and Joseph stayed close by, no doubt ready to offer an arm if she stumbled. "I bet it's spectacular when finished."

Thick white crown molding framed the front door which stood partially open, revealing the beginnings of a staircase. Beautiful. This was exactly what Charlotte had envisioned when making her proposals back in Durham for her own school.

She stumbled over a dirt clod and threw out her hands to steady herself. "I'm okay," she said, motioning Joseph and Karla back.

"I hope they put in sidewalks soon," Emma said, grabbing Charlotte's arm for support. "This walk is positively treacherous."

An exaggeration, but Charlotte loved Emma for the subtle dig at Adam.

"It's definitely on our production schedule," said a deep voice.

Charlotte jumped, putting a hand to her chest. When had Adam shown up? He stood in the doorway, a silhouette back-lit by the morning sun. Charlotte took a few steps closer and realized he held two hard hats.

The front steps hadn't been poured yet, and Charlotte accepted Joseph's helping hand onto the front porch. She smoothed down her skirt, smiling at Adam.

He'd been so kind to Karabo last night. She couldn't forget that, even if she wanted to.

"Good morning," she said pleasantly.

"Morning." Adam extended hard hats to them. "Welcome to the School Montgomery."

Charlotte drew back, staring at the hat. It was a crisp white, but had a band just inside that would destroy the curls she'd spent so much time on that morning. And just what kind of heads had this hat been on? "You have got to be kidding me."

Adam smirked. "This is a construction site, Princess. We can't have a piece of drywall landing on your head."

She took back every nice thought she'd had about him yesterday at the welcome dinner. Maybe he had been kind to Karabo, but he was clearly tormenting her. "There is no way I'm putting that hat anywhere near my body."

"It's brand new and squeaky clean," Adam said. "I personally disinfected it myself."

"No." Charlotte shook her head back and forth. "Not happening."

"I'm afraid I must insist, Princess," Joseph said in his gruff voice. "We can't allow you into the building without it."

Charlotte folded her arms and glared at Joseph. "I thought you were supposed to be on my side."

"Oh, come on, Char." Emma took her own hat and placed it on her head, then struck a pose. "How do I look?"

"Like someone who's about to get head lice," Charlotte said.

Emma rolled her eyes. "Adam said they're brand new, and besides, he wouldn't let that happen to us. Can you imagine the headlines? Not very good publicity for his school."

"Her Highness is right," Adam said. But there was a twinkle in his eye that made Charlotte raise one eyebrow doubtfully.

She eyed the hat, still not accepting it. It wasn't that she'd never worn a hard hat before—of course she had—but Becky usually prepped her beforehand so she could choose a hairstyle that wouldn't look ridiculous in photos. "I don't know."

"If you end up with some infectious disease, I give you permission to punish me in whatever way you see fit." Adam took a step toward her, pushing the hat into her hands. When he spoke next, his voice was low and flirtatious. "Just another side effect of being a princess, right?"

Charlotte snatched the hat away, her heart beating rapidly in her chest. Before she could think too much about it, she plopped the hat on her head. No bad odors reached her nose, which had to be a good sign, but the weight of the hat was unfamiliar and awkward. "There. Happy?"

"Undoubtedly."

Emma headed inside, and Charlotte followed. "I look ridiculous," she muttered as she brushed past Adam.

His eyes ran up and down her figure, sending a thrill of excitement through her stomach which she tried to squelch.

"You look beautiful," Adam said. He cleared his throat, motioning with one arm. "If you'll head down the hallway, Blessing is waiting with the rest of the group in what will eventually be the front office. Just follow the noise and you can't miss it. I'll be along as soon as the last few people arrive."

The hallway was open. Wooden studs outlined where it would eventually run, but no drywall yet defined the space and Charlotte could see into each of the rooms.

As they headed toward the front office, Emma murmured, "The two of you are awful chummy today. What's up with that?"

"We were arguing," Charlotte hissed.

"That's what I'm talking about. There was a definite heat between the two of you." Emma scowled. "I don't like it."

"If Adam can be civil, then so can I."

"As long as you remember that he's a two-timing snake," Emma said.

"We never agreed to be exclusive." Although, after that last night spent kissing beneath the stars on his balcony, Charlotte had certainly wanted to be.

Emma flipped her dark hair over one shoulder, then adjusted her hard hat. "It's kind of implied when you're dating a princess."

The murmur of voices grew louder as they approached the end of the hall. This room was drywalled, and Charlotte entered with a gasp.

Blessing waited in the middle of the room with half a dozen other people. She lifted a hand in a wave and said, "Welcome."

"Thank you," Charlotte said, trying not to openly gawk at the room. The drywall had been hung, all right. But it had also been destroyed.

"Whoa," Emma murmured, looking around.

"No kidding," Charlotte whispered back. It looked as though someone had taken an ax to the room. Deep slashes cut through every sheet of drywall. Some panels were missing entirely, while others featured large holes, as though someone had put a foot through them.

"I was just explaining to the others that we had a bit of a situation with some vandals a couple of nights back and haven't quite gotten it all cleaned up yet."

Blessing clasped her hands together, her smile forced. "But not to worry. We have everything under control, and will soon be back on track."

"Such a shame," one of the professors said, shaking his head.

Two more people entered the room then—government officials Charlotte recognized from last night's dinner—and Blessing began her explanation once more.

"Surely they have security guards keeping this place safe at night," Charlotte muttered out of the corner of her mouth.

"Obviously not," Emma said. "How could this much destruction happen without drawing their attention?"

Three more people arrived, dressed in traditional African clothing. The delegates from the tribe, perhaps? Whoever they were, they didn't look very happy to be here. The tall, elegant woman with dark skin held a beautiful red izicolo hat in her hands, since the hard hat was on her head. She caught Charlotte's eye and frowned. Charlotte gave a quick smile, feeling embarrassed, but the woman merely blinked and turned away.

Adam strode into the room then, adjusting the cufflinks on his light beige suit. How did he manage to always look so fantastic? She could see the blue color of his eyes even from across the room, and the sharply cut jaw made her knees turn to liquid.

"Welcome," he said, going to stand next to Blessing. "Blessing and I are so excited to show you around the School Montgomery this morning. If you didn't have a chance to meet her last night, she's the director of this wonderful institution."

"It looks like you're running into some difficulties here," one of the professors said in a thick German accent.

Blessing's hands were fluttering near her stomach, and she shot Adam a panicked glance.

"It's true that we've had a few incidents with vandalism recently, but I think you'll still be able to see today how much progress we've made here," Adam said smoothly. "Blessing, why don't you tell them about this room?"

Blessing nodded, her hands still twitching. Adam's words from Durham flashed suddenly into Charlotte's mind. *"I fear she's cracking up,"* Adam had said. *"She's got the qualifications, but I'm not sure if she's up to the stress of the job."* It seemed his worry was founded, because Blessing had seemed on edge last night, too.

"Right now, we stand in what will eventually be the front office area of the school," Blessing said. "The school is designed for two hundred and ten students, although we expect our numbers to be about half that the first year—perhaps somewhere around one hundred and twenty students. The School Montgomery is unique in that it will provide a free education to any local tribe child between the ages of five and eighteen who wishes to attend."

"And what if their parents do not wish their child to attend the school?" the woman holding the izicolo asked, lifting her chin. "Many of our tribe wish to continue teaching their children at home, where we can be assured they are learning our values."

That was to be expected, Charlotte supposed. She'd attended enough education conferences to know that attempts to increase educational opportunities were often met with resistance by the very people those opportunities would benefit. But from Emma's raised eyebrows, Charlotte guessed her cousin didn't know this.

"Attendance is not compulsory," Blessing said, her voice a pitch higher than it had been before. She glanced over at Adam, who gave an encouraging nod. "We will educate any student who wishes to learn."

"That does not answer my question," the woman said. "Some of my tribe are worried that if a child wishes to attend, but the parent does not approve, that child may be educated against the parent's wishes."

"Parental permission will be required for any child to enroll."

"And what if one parent agrees, and the other does not?" the woman pressed.

"The logistics of enrollment are still being worked out," Blessing said, her voice cracking. She motioned toward the door. "If you'll follow me, we can head upstairs to view the classrooms. There will be ten in all, once the school is finished. Some grades may be combined into one class, depending on our enrollment numbers. Which classes to combine, or not combine, is something we will continually reevaluate each year as the student population fluctuates . . ."

Charlotte watched Adam, but he seemed content to let Blessing take the lead as she showed them around the second floor, only jumping in when she seemed distressed. Charlotte had to give him credit for letting the woman do her job, despite her obvious nerves. The delegates from the tribe kept up a continual stream of accusatory questions, not making Blessing's task easy.

Signs of vandalism were subtle, but nearly everywhere they turned. Words in a language Charlotte didn't recognize were spray painted on the particle board floor. As they passed by one of the classrooms, Charlotte noticed it was dark. Strange, since all the others were lit. Had the wiring perhaps been cut?

"What happened here?" she murmured to Emma as they headed back downstairs.

"I'm no expert when it comes to construction, but this place seems way behind schedule," Emma said.

Charlotte had to agree. Would it really be ready by September?

Back on the first floor, Blessing motioned to an open space. "And this will be the cafeteria."

Charlotte glanced through the open studs, trying to visualize the space. The exterior walls were still covered in half-destroyed drywall, which made it difficult to imagine the happy chatter of kids as they sat together eating lunch.

"It can hold up to one hundred and thirty students at a time, which allows us to easily feed the entire school in two shifts once we've reached maximum capacity," Blessing continued. "We are very excited to announce that we recently obtained a grant, which will allow us to provide breakfast and lunch free of charge to all students on every school day."

Emma adjusted her hard hat, looking bored, but Charlotte was impressed. She knew from working with other schools just how challenging providing meals could be.

"Our children do not need to be fed your processed foods while they receive what you deem a proper education."

The speaker was the man in African robes who had kept close to the woman with the izicolo hat the entire tour. Charlotte wasn't certain, but she thought they might be relatives of some sort. He wore white linen pants and a bright blue tunic that reached nearly to his knees, the scowl on his face at odds with his colorful clothing.

Adam folded his arms, watching the man with an unreadable expression. Next to him, Blessing's hands had clenched into fists at her sides.

"Perhaps you have forgotten that we are here because of an agreement with the local tribes," Blessing said. "The school is intended for—"

"Lies!" the woman screamed, shaking her hat at Blessing.

The room erupted into a flurry of voices.

A hand wrapped firmly around Charlotte's arm, and she glanced up at Joseph.

"Time to go," he said, pulling her forward.

In moments, Charlotte and Emma were shut inside the car, headed back toward the hotel. Karla sat beside Charlotte, her face grim, while Joseph occupied the front passenger seat.

"Sorry about that situation, Your Highnesses," Joseph said. "We never suspected things might turn hostile."

Emma shook her head, as though she couldn't process what had just occurred.

Charlotte understood the feeling. "What in the world happened back there?"

Joseph didn't answer. He had a hand pressed to his ear, obviously listening to something being said on his earpiece. Then he said, "Yes, check the entire hotel again. We'll head back to Durham if you find anything amiss."

"What?" Charlotte demanded, her heart beating rapidly in her chest. She turned to Emma. "Did he really just say that?"

Emma lifted her hands in a helpless shrug.

Charlotte shook Joseph's shoulder roughly. "Tell me what's going on."

She couldn't go back to Durham. Panic clawed at her as she thought of going home now. She wasn't done in South Africa. She hadn't obtained closure, whatever that meant.

Wait. Had she come here for closure—answers to questions only Adam could give?

She swallowed hard, sinking back against her seat. This wasn't about Adam, it was about the conference. So many professionals had come to hear her speak at this conference, and she didn't want to disappoint them by canceling at the last moment.

Joseph turned in his chair, looking directly at Charlotte. "It appears the tensions between the tribe and the school have escalated. Your safety is my first priority."

"But the speech—"

"You'll still be able to give it, provided we don't turn up anything concerning," Joseph said. "But I'm sorry, Your Highness. If something happens, we're gone."

"He's right, Char," Emma said quietly. "Giant arguments on school tours weren't part of the deal when you agreed to come."

Charlotte pulled out her phone with trembling hands. She scrolled to a contact she hadn't used in months, staring at the name. It simply said *A*. She hadn't wanted to give away too much if someone looked at her phone.

What just happened in there? she texted. Then she took a deep breath and pushed *send*.

The ride back to the hotel was only five minutes, but her anxiety made it last an eternity. Joseph and Karla stayed close as they escorted them to the suite, not relaxing until the door was securely closed behind them.

"Well, that was exciting," Emma said breezily, pulling off her hard hat and fluffing her hair. Charlotte had completely forgotten they were still wearing the hats. "I'm going to slip into my suit and go for a swim in the pool. Want to come?"

"I'm not sure that's wise, Your Highness," Joseph said.

Emma waved a hand lazily. "The hot tub on the balcony then. Char?"

"Sure," she said numbly, reaching up to pull off her own hat. "Give me five minutes."

Emma nodded and disappeared into her room. Charlotte did the same, closing the door firmly behind her.

She wasn't ready to go home. Something about South Africa made her feel independent and happy and free.

Maybe it's because Adam's here, a small voice whispered at the back of her mind. But she batted that away.

Her phone buzzed, and she fumbled to pull it from her clutch.

Adam had texted back just three words: **Where are you?**

Her fingers flew across the screen. **Back at the hotel. We were whisked out of there when the arguing began.**

Sorry about that.

What happened?

Charlotte stared at her phone, willing a response. A moment later, it buzzed again.

It's a long story, Adam said. **Can I drop by your suite when I get back to the hotel? I'll explain everything then.**

Charlotte stared at the phone, the significance of the request weighing on her. He was asking permission to drop by. If she said yes, that would be like . . . well, she didn't know what that would be like.

What was going on with the school? In Durham, he'd mentioned they'd run into a few problems trying to get the school opened. But she'd had no idea that things were so bad.

I suppose so, she texted back. **But I want to know everything.**

Deal. It might be an hour or two before I can get there.

That was enough time to relax in the hot tub with Emma and hopefully clear her head.

I'll be waiting, she said. Then she went to change into her swimsuit.

Chapter Eight

Adam leaned forward, resting his arms on his desk as he stared at Blessing. The hum of the air conditioner filled the room, counteracting the sun streaming through his open windows.

The last hour had lasted an eternity. Adam hadn't even noticed that Charlotte and Emma had disappeared until he got her text. He was too busy trying to calm the tempers of everyone present and restore order to the tour.

Adam had tried to usher the tribe delegates into another room, hoping he could assuage their fears without an audience. Not that there were a lot of options for privacy, since the construction crew had to remove most of the damaged drywall. But in the end, the delegates had stormed from the school, yelling something in a language that Adam didn't understand.

With Keith's help, Adam had been able to shrug off the incident and convince the other members of the tour to return to the Hotel Montgomery for the first workshop of the day. He'd asked Blessing to accompany him back to the hotel and texted Charlotte on the drive back. Keith must have told Brionna about the incident, because she was waiting for Adam in his office when he arrived with Blessing.

"Please don't quit," Adam said. "At least, not right now. No one wants you to make a permanent decision after such a stressful morning."

Blessing folded her arms tightly across her chest and pressed her lips together. She was staring fixedly at the clock above Adam's desk, not meeting his eyes. "I'm sorry, Mr. Montgomery. I know this puts you in a bind. But that argument with the tribe delegates really put things in perspective for me."

In his peripheral vision, Adam saw Brionna shift in her chair. "I understand that emotions were extremely high back at the school. But I think once we—"

Blessing was already shaking her head, hands fluttering near her throat. "No. I refuse to deal with this anymore. Lately, I'm upset all the time. I've even started to lose my hair." She motioned to the tight bun at the base of her skull. "Do you see how thin it's getting? I can't keep sacrificing my health for this job, especially when there are no signs that things will improve."

"Of course we don't expect you to sacrifice your health," Adam said. "I'd never ask that of you. But surely we can reach some sort of compromise?"

Brionna nodded at Adam approvingly. Blessing was still staring steadfastly at the clock, refusing to look at either of them.

"I know today was hard," Brionna said, "but you are more than capable of doing this job. Think of all the good we're trying to accomplish here. Generations of the tribe's children will learn to read and write, and it will all be thanks to you."

Blessing finally looked at Brionna, and that's when Adam knew he'd lost. Blessing's jaw was set, her eyes brimming with tears.

"The tribe doesn't want the school," Blessing said. "And who are we to force it on them? You don't understand the dynamics at play here, Miss Cartwright. I've spent my entire life in South Africa. Those delegates today genuinely fear that we're trying to destroy their culture."

"But you know that's wrong, and I know that's wrong," Brionna said, her tone soft and soothing. "If the tribe as a whole didn't want the school, then why would Chief Mandla have put it in the contract? It's only a few people who are upset by what we're doing."

But it was over. Adam took a deep breath, accepting defeat. "Email me an official resignation letter and copy human resources on it. I'll make sure they send you your final check by the end of the week."

Blessing quickly brushed away the tears that trailed down her cheeks and rose. "Thank you, Mr. Montgomery. I'm sorry this is how it had to end."

"Me too." Adam reached across the desk and extended his hand, trying to keep the bitterness from his voice. "Best of luck."

Blessing nodded and quickly left the room.

Brionna waited until the door clicked shut, then turned to Adam, her eyes flashing. "Why did you let her leave? We can't open the school by September first without her."

Adam rubbed his eyes, feeling suddenly weary. He didn't want to have this conversation with Brionna. "We were wasting our breath trying to get her to stay. We need someone as invested in the school as we are, and Blessing isn't that person."

"You can't oversee every aspect of this project yourself, Adam. Where are you going to find another school director on such short notice, much less a qualified one?"

He hated when Brionna spoke to him like this— like he was a naïve child who couldn't grasp the consequences of his actions. "I'll figure it out."

"Before or after the tribe sues Montgomery Hotels & Resorts?" Brionna leaned forward, placing her hands flat on his desk. "It's not just your name on the line anymore. If Montgomery plans to enter into business with Cartwright hotels, you can't let this happen."

Ah yes, the merger between their two hotel empires that Brionna kept hinting at. Adam knew he should take a clear step toward defining their relationship. Marrying Brionna made perfect business sense. But he couldn't get Charlotte out of his mind.

She'd texted him today. It was the first time she'd initiated contact since he'd returned to South Africa. That had to mean something.

He shouldn't want it to mean anything.

"Take a deep breath," Adam told Brionna. "You're starting to spiral."

She closed her eyes, inhaling sharply. "You're right. Sorry. I just know my father will never allow us to enter into business together if Montgomery gets caught up in a scandal. We could be so good together, Adam. Think of what a legacy we'd leave behind if we merged our two empires."

It sounded so clinical when she spoke of it—a merger, not a marriage. Adam rested his chin on his hand, watching Brionna. Why did she want this merger to happen so badly?

"The Montgomerys want to avoid a scandal just as much as the Cartwrights do," Adam said finally. "The hotel is doing great right now and I'm not going to let the school ruin that."

Brionna's eyes were narrowed, but she finally gave a sharp nod. "Well, what's done is done. Where are we going to find a new director on such short notice?"

"I don't know." Adam glanced at his watch, muttering a curse. "I'll see if Keith can post the job opening on the hotel's website—that's the best I can do right now. I'm late for another meeting, and then I need to make sure everything is ready for Her Highness's keynote speech this evening. Sorry to run off like this."

But Brionna didn't make a move to leave. Instead, she tapped a finger against her lips, eyes unfocused.

"Brionna?"

"It just occurred to me who the perfect candidate for the job is," Brionna said slowly.

That was good news. Adam rose, grabbing his suit coat off the back of his chair and shrugging into it. "Anyone I know?"

"Yes. Princess Charlotte would be perfect for this."

Adam stopped adjusting his jacket, staring at Brionna. "You have got to be kidding me."

Brionna rose as well, her eyes bright. "It's perfect, Adam. Her Highness is extremely passionate about education."

"Yeah. And she's also a princess." Adam grabbed his cell phone off the desk, checking for any texts from Charlotte—there were none—before dropping it in his pocket. "I don't think she's looking for a job."

"So don't tell her it's a job—tell her it's a goodwill opportunity. I know she's been heavily involved in other school openings in the past. Maybe, with her on board, the tribe will stop harassing us and we can finally get back on schedule."

Adam leaned against his desk, folding his arms. "There are more than three months left on the project. It would be impossible for her to stay away from Durham for that long."

"How do you know unless you ask? You're an earl. Don't members of the nobility have some sort of code in Durham?"

"I'm not earl yet."

Brionna waved a hand. "Whatever. Adam, this is perfect. Princess Charlotte is incredibly influential. She'll bring a notoriety and prestige to the project that's been lacking. I think the vandalism might stop if she's on board. Surely whoever is doing the vandalism wouldn't dare go up against a princess."

"I really don't think the people punching holes in the drywall will care." Adam brushed a piece of lint off his jacket, then headed toward the door. "I'll have Keith put in a request with Edgemont Security for new guards at the site. Maybe you're right about them being bribed into silence."

Brionna grabbed Adam by the arm, stopping him just inside the doorway.

"You should at least ask her," Brionna said. "What's the worst that can happen?"

She had no idea. But Adam said, "I'll think about it." And then he headed to Charlotte's suite.

Chapter Nine

"*I* can't believe you asked him to come here," Emma said, her eyes closed as she rested her head against the back of the hot tub. The hum of the jets overpowered the chirp of birds, and a gentle breeze played with the steam rising from the waters.

Charlotte adjusted so that one of the jets hit the knot on her back that had been bothering her for days. She let out a contented sigh. "Aren't you curious about what happened at the school?"

"Sure, but I don't think inviting your ex to your room is the best way to handle that curiosity."

Charlotte wanted to roll her eyes, but she was too relaxed. "You make it sound so salacious. All I want is answers. Considering I just flew all the way to South Africa for a keynote speech I might not even be allowed to give, I think I deserve at least that much."

"Joseph said all the security sweeps came up clean, so I think they'll let you give the speech tonight. Whatever is going on, it isn't about us. It doesn't even seem to be about the hotel. I guess some people just really don't want that school."

"That's what I want to find out," Charlotte said.

"Well, I'm not leaving you alone with Adam. You two were standing just a little too close for my liking when I found you last night."

This time, Charlotte did roll her eyes. But she didn't argue, because Emma was right—Adam was reeling Charlotte back in. And she couldn't let that happen.

"Ten more minutes?" Emma asked.

"Definitely." Charlotte let the warm water soothe the stress from her muscles. She had seriously underestimated the medicinal properties of a hot tub. When she got back to Durham, she was ordering one of these for the palace.

Charlotte had dried off and changed clothes, and was just twisting her hair into an elegant chignon—the hard hat had completely flattened the curls she'd spent thirty minutes on that morning—when a knock sounded at the door.

Emma grabbed a magazine off the coffee table and sank deliberately onto the couch, resting her feet on the cushions so that she took up the entire space. She motioned meaningfully to the two chairs across from her. "Don't want you two getting too cozy."

"This is completely unnecessary," Charlotte said as Karla walked into the room.

Karla paused, motioning to the door. "Should I not answer it?"

"I was talking to Emma," Charlotte said.

Karla nodded, and a moment later Adam was let into the suite. He was still in the same light-colored suit from earlier, but his shirt was definitely more wrinkled than before, and his face was tight with stress.

"Hey," Charlotte said, motioning him toward one of the two empty chairs. "Please, sit down."

"Thank you." Adam settled into the chair, giving Emma a quick nod. "Your Highness."

She barely looked up from her magazine and lazily flipped a page. "Mr. Montgomery."

Karla disappeared from the room, but Charlotte knew she and Joseph would remain nearby.

Charlotte took the last empty seat, remaining on the edge of the cushion with her back straight. "So," she said, looking at Adam. His jaw was clenched, and she longed to run a hand along it and will him to relax. But that was no longer her right. "Are you going to tell me what happened today?"

Adam ran a hand through his hair, then over his jaw. His eyes flicked to Emma, then back to Charlotte. "Yes. But it's a long story."

Charlotte clasped her hands in her lap, giving him her full attention. "I have nowhere to be until my keynote address. I'm listening."

Adam nodded. "You already know that some members of the tribe aren't thrilled about the school."

Charlotte flinched at the reference to the time they'd spent together in secret. She struggled to control her face, not wanting Adam to read the emotions flowing through her. "Yes, but you never said things were so bad."

"I didn't want to worry you." He shook his head, wincing. "No, that's a lie. I didn't want you to think me incompetent at my job."

Her heart lurched, and she reached a hand toward Adam. But Emma cleared her throat loudly just then, and Charlotte snatched it back.

"I would never think that," Charlotte said. "You should have told me. Maybe I could have helped."

"Maybe." Adam leaned forward, resting his arms on his knees and clasping his hands together. "We started having issues at the construction site almost as soon as we broke ground. Tools would go missing, equipment would mysteriously break, that sort of thing. So I hired security guards to keep an eye on the place at night. That seemed to stop the problems, for a while at least. But ever since my return from Durham, things have escalated again. Now the tribe's council is threatening to sue for breach of contract if we don't open the school by September first. We're already nearly a year behind schedule, but they've been lenient up until now, given the circumstances."

Pain flashed across Adam's face at the reminder of his mother's death, and Charlotte ached to comfort him. Instead, she clasped her hands more tightly together, wishing she had a book between them.

It wasn't her job anymore to comfort Adam. She'd invited him here for answers, and that's what she intended to get. "Why did the delegates from the tribe come on the tour if they don't approve of the school?"

"I'm guessing Chief Mandla prodded them into attending. He's the one who turned down our initial offer for the land. We offered him fifteen percent above market value, but he wanted the school instead."

Adam ran a hand over his jaw, drawing Charlotte's attention. She bit her lip and looked away, swallowing hard. She must not think about what it felt like to kiss him.

"The chief has been extremely understanding and helpful through this entire process, and most of the members of the council want the school, too—the contract never would have been signed if a majority hadn't voted for it. But unfortunately, there's a very vocal minority against the school, and they seem determined to make sure it's never built."

Emma turned another page of her magazine, the quiet *swish* of paper somehow loud in the silence. Charlotte's mind whirled with this new information. Adam had, of course, told her about the school during their time together in Durham. One evening, after watching a movie about a teacher in an inner-city school, Charlotte had confessed to him just how badly she wanted to open a school in Castlebridge. She knew it would probably never happen—not with the opposition from her mother. But Adam had been encouraging of the idea and mentioned that the Hotel Montgomery was building a school just a mile from their resort.

"So yeah, that's the story." Adam blew out a breath. "Today was the last straw for Blessing. She finally quit, right before I came up here. That's what took me so long. I was trying to talk her into staying, but it didn't work."

"She quit?" Charlotte said in disbelief. "But September first is barely three months away."

"I know."

"What are you going to do?"

"Hire a new director, I suppose." Adam glanced at her, then quickly away again, his eyes flickering back toward Emma. "I'm really sorry you had to see that today. I've never seen the delegates from the tribe so angry before, but I guess something about the tour rubbed them the wrong way."

"I suppose so," Charlotte said. What was Adam not saying?

"Hopefully your speech tonight will help them see how good the school can be for their children."

"Thanks a lot. No pressure or anything."

"You'll do great. You always do." Adam pushed to his feet. "Thanks for listening to me. I'd better go make sure everything is ready for tonight. I know your security detail had some concerns, but I think the hotel security has managed to assure them you're perfectly safe."

Charlotte rose as well, walking with Adam to the door. "I think so. Joseph said I can still talk tonight, as long as nothing changes."

"Good." Adam paused in the entryway, taking a step toward Charlotte.

She swallowed, glancing toward the living room. But the entryway was recessed enough that it blocked most of the living room, and Charlotte couldn't see Emma on the couch. She and Adam were alone—relatively speaking.

"You're a remarkable woman, Charlotte Somerset," Adam murmured. "I know whatever you say tonight will completely captivate the audience."

Charlotte bit her lip, taking a step back. She bumped into the wall and pressed her hands flat against it. "I don't know about that."

His hand caressed her cheek, the touch so soft that she wondered if she'd imagined it. Adam cleared his throat, rubbing a hand over his jaw. "Well, you've always captivated me. See you tonight?"

"Tonight," Charlotte agreed.

Adam nodded and left the room. Charlotte closed the door behind him and leaned against it, her knees suddenly weak.

He'd touched her cheek. Why had he done that? Brionna was staying at his hotel. That had to mean they were together now.

Charlotte slowly walked back into the living room. Emma had abandoned her magazine and moved her feet back to the floor, so Charlotte sank down on the couch beside her cousin.

"Well, that was awfully cozy," Emma said.

Charlotte gave a weak smile. Could Emma hear the pounding of her heart? "I guess things are more complicated with the school than we realized."

"That's not what I'm talking about. He's playing you, Char."

"What do you mean?"

Emma chewed her lip. "The flirting, the overly solicitous behavior . . . I don't know. Something smells rotten. That's all I'm saying."

"He was just answering my questions."

"And struggling to keep his hands to himself the entire time. You two would have been all over each other if I hadn't been in the room."

"Not true," Charlotte shot back.

Emma rose, heading to the sidebar and selecting an apple from the fruit basket. "I just don't want to see you get hurt again."

"I'm not going to," Charlotte said. "In two days, we'll be back in Durham, right?"

Emma pointed a finger at Charlotte. "Right. And don't you forget it."

Chapter Ten

Charlotte nervously smoothed down the folds of her dress, gazing at the stairs leading up to the stage. *Please don't let me trip,* she silently begged. Even after a lifetime of lessons in grace, every time the spotlight shone on Charlotte she vividly remembered the time she was ten and tripped on the red carpet of a movie premier. The photographers had caught the moment, and the images had circulated for months.

Adam's deep voice boomed across the sound system, listing off a string of Charlotte's accomplishments. But even after years of advocating for education, Charlotte still felt like a fraud. Why should anyone care what she had to say? She paced in front of the steps, clutching her notes in both hands as she mentally ran through her speech for the thousandth time. She'd memorized most of it, but tended to freeze in front of crowds so she always kept a hard copy close by, just in case.

Two hundred and thirty-seven people were in the audience, waiting to hear her speak. Charlotte wondered if any of the dissenters from the tribe were present. Would they be rude enough to interrupt her address? She didn't think so, but after what had happened at the school, she wasn't sure. Heavens, this day had lasted an eternity. She couldn't believe that had only been about nine hours ago.

Emma leaned against one wall, watching Charlotte as she paced.

"You'll do great," Emma said encouragingly. "It'll all be over before you know it, and tomorrow morning Becky has scheduled in a safari tour. That'll make this all worth it, right?"

Charlotte gave a short nod. No one in the family particularly enjoyed giving speeches, but Charlotte always felt like her nerves showed, whereas the others came across as so composed.

"It is with great honor that we welcome to the stage Her Royal Highness Princess Charlotte of Durham," Adam said, his voice booming through the microphone.

Charlotte froze, her hands clammy. The polite clapping of two hundred and thirty-seven people filtered to where she waited at the bottom of the stairs.

"Good luck," Emma whispered.

Charlotte took a deep breath, then ascended the stage. The spotlights blinded her, but she'd given enough speeches to expect that—welcomed it, even. It was easier to pretend no one was there when she couldn't make out their faces.

She put on her best princess smile and waved to the nearly invisible crowd. Her dress was a trumpet-cut and her heels exceptionally tall, which made walking difficult. But she kept her chin high and tried to exude confidence, just as her decorum tutor Mrs. Grant had always instructed her and Emma to do. As teenagers, they'd spent hours practicing walking in every silhouette of gown imaginable while Mrs. Grant critiqued their every move.

Adam stood next to the podium, that knee-melting smile on his face as he clapped along with the others. He held out a hand, and she took it, letting him help her the last few steps. His grip was firm but gentle, just like his kisses.

She quickly let go of his hand and took a shaky breath, keeping her smile in place.

"Thank you, Mr. Montgomery, for that most flattering introduction," Charlotte said as Adam exited the stage. She turned to the crowd. "Today, we are here to speak about something that is of the utmost importance . . ."

Unlike her brothers, Charlotte always wrote her own speeches. The words flowed easily, and she felt herself growing more and more passionate with every passing moment. Cameras flashed as she spoke about the improvements she'd helped make to Durham's public education system. She was dimly aware of the stray coughs that echoed through the room and the shuffle of feet against carpet as the audience adjusted positions. Either the delegates from the tribe weren't present, or they were behaving respectfully, because no one interrupted Charlotte.

She glanced down at her notes, moving on to stories of the schools she'd consulted on in various parts of the world. The difficulties Adam's school was experiencing played through her mind, and something inside her burned to help. The School Montgomery might no longer have a director, and it might be behind schedule, but surely there was something that could be done to ensure it opened on time.

"We may think our actions don't matter," Charlotte said, looking over the crowd. The spotlights still mostly blinded her, but her eyes had adjusted and she could make out the individual shapes of people now. "But like a drop of water in a pond, those actions can create a ripple effect that will impact generations yet to come. Thank you."

Thunderous applause filled the room. First one person, then two, then a dozen rose to their feet, until the entire room stood. Tears of gratitude and appreciation welled in Charlotte's eyes, and she quickly blinked them back. She lifted a hand in thanks, then gathered her notes and made her way off the stage and down the stairs to where she was once again safely hidden from the audience's eyes.

Emma waited at the bottom of the stairs, her eyes glowing. She immediately pulled Charlotte into a fierce hug. "That was amazing, Char. They loved you!"

Charlotte shook out her hands, laughing, as they walked into the hallway. The door swung shut behind them, deadening the sound of Adam closing the session. "I'm so glad that's over. I feel all sweaty from nerves."

"You don't look it."

"Were delegates from the tribe in the audience?"

"I didn't see any, but it's pretty packed in there. Everyone was hanging on your every word." Emma laughed, nudging Charlotte's shoulder. "No one ever pays that close of attention when I speak."

"Not true," Charlotte said. "But it was very inspiring to see everyone's passion for education and literacy. We should see if we can get the royal family to donate books to the library for when the school opens."

"Excellent idea," Emma said.

Adam appeared in the hallway then, a broad smile on his face. He strode over and crushed her to him in a hug.

Charlotte's arms wrapped around his waist of their own accord, and she inhaled the spicy scent of his cologne.

"You were brilliant in there," Adam whispered, his breath tickling her cheek.

She closed her eyes, pain mixing with euphoria at his touch. Brionna could walk in at any moment. Charlotte shouldn't be hugging another girl's boyfriend this tightly.

Someone cleared their throat loudly—Emma, no doubt—and Charlotte reluctantly stepped back.

"Thanks," she said. "I'm just glad it's over."

"They loved you," Adam said. His expression darkened. "I just wish the delegates from the tribe had been here to hear it."

Disappointment cut at Charlotte's happiness, and she realized that she'd wanted them to hear her speech, too. Maybe, if they'd heard the stories of other villages she'd helped, they wouldn't be so reluctant to have the School Montgomery teaching their own children. "No one came from the tribe?"

"Just Chief Mandla and his wife," Adam said. "Come on, I want to introduce you to him."

Adam wrapped Charlotte's hand in his, tugging her down the hallway. She passed by a glaring Emma, feeling bewildered. Why was Adam being so affectionate? Charlotte held his hand tightly with her own, realizing with horror that she never wanted to stop.

What was happening?

Adam dropped her hand the moment they entered the ballroom, and Charlotte immediately felt its loss. She swallowed, feeling disoriented. The chatter of attendees discussing the day's classes bounced off the coffered ceilings.

"Excellent address, Your Highness," someone said as Charlotte followed Adam through the room.

"I don't remember the last time I enjoyed a keynote so much," someone else said.

"Thank you," Charlotte stammered, smiling as she accepted the congratulations of those nearby.

Adam rested his hand at the small of Charlotte's back, propelling her gently forward and smiling at those offering their praise.

"See?" he murmured near her ear. "I told you they loved you. And I can't say that I blame them."

What did that mean?

Adam tapped the shoulder of a tall man wearing an impeccably cut suit. The man turned around, smiling broadly down at them. His head was completely bald, the chandelier prisms casting rainbows across his dark skin, and his face clean shaven.

"Chief Mandla," Adam said, holding an arm out to Charlotte. "There's someone I'd like you to meet."

"Princess Charlotte," Chief Mandla said before Adam could introduce her. He reached out, taking Charlotte's hand carefully in his own, and bowed low over it. "It is a great honor to meet you this evening."

"The honor is mine, Chief Mandla," Charlotte said.

"This is my wife, Londiwe," the chief said, motioning to the woman beside him. She was pretty, with dark skin, pretty eyes, and a dark red izicolo on her head. "Please excuse her silence—she does not speak English."

The woman gave Charlotte a wide, happy smile, which Charlotte returned.

"We both very much enjoyed your address tonight," Mandla said. "We had a translator join us so Londiwe could hear it, too. Both my wife and I have long admired your efforts to bring educational opportunities to disadvantaged parts of the world."

Adam gave Charlotte a smile brimming with pride. "Her Highness is a remarkable woman."

The praise warmed Charlotte's heart, thawing some of the ice that Adam had left behind. Why was he doing this to her?

"Thank you. That really means a lot to me." Charlotte fought the urge to brush her hair behind one ear—a nervous habit Mrs. Grant had spent years breaking her of. "It's an honor to help in any way that I can."

"We are glad to hear that," Chief Mandla said, clasping his hands together. "Perhaps you have heard of the difficulties we've encountered in getting our school built here?"

Charlotte nodded. "I'm so sorry about the vandalism that's put things behind schedule."

"As are we," the man said. "This school is very important to the children in my tribe, even if some refuse to see it."

"Have you tried holding a public forum at the village?" Charlotte asked. "Representatives from the school would do a presentation, and then members of the tribe could ask questions and voice any concerns they may have. I've seen it done quite effectively in similar situations."

Chief Mandla's eyes lit up, and he turned to Adam. "That's an excellent idea."

"I agree," Adam said. "I'll have Keith contact you sometime this week to set things in motion."

Mandla chuckled, patting Charlotte's hand. "I knew you would be good for us, Your Highness. Are you sure you don't want to stick around?"

Charlotte laughed, shaking her head. "South Africa is beautiful, but I must return to Durham for my brother's wedding."

"A shame," Chief Mandla said. "Perhaps one day our paths will cross again, Your Highness."

"I hope so," Charlotte said. "It was a pleasure meeting you."

"You as well." Mandla gave one last low bow, then strode away, Londiwe following close behind him.

"He seems like a very nice man," Charlotte said.

Adam nodded. "Chief Mandla has been invaluable during this mess with the school, but his influence only extends so far. He has an idea who the vandals might be, but so far we haven't found any evidence, and no one's confessing."

"Maybe having an open house will help."

"Maybe. It's definitely a good idea that we're going to try."

"What's a good idea?" a high, feminine voice asked.

Charlotte turned around, feeling the tension leak into her shoulders. Brionna. She looked back and forth between Adam and Charlotte, wearing the same plastic smile on her lips that she always had in pictures. Charlotte took a careful step away from Adam, hoping Brionna hadn't noticed just how closely they were standing.

"Her Highness suggested we hold an open house for the tribes," Adam said. "Maybe if we give them a chance to express their concerns, we can figure out a way to help them feel comfortable with the school."

Brionna's smile grew even wider, something Charlotte hadn't thought was possible. "What a good idea. Oh, I'm so glad you've agreed to help us with the school. We really need your expertise during these last few months of construction. I'm sure we need to start hiring teachers soon, but I have no idea where to even begin."

Charlotte held up a hand, and Brionna quieted. "Wait. What did you say about helping the school?"

Brionna glanced over at Adam, and Charlotte turned just in time to see him frantically shaking his head.

"Adam didn't tell you?" Brionna asked, her brow pulled together in confusion. "We want you to be the interim director of the school."

Chapter Eleven

$\mathcal{A}$dam stared at Brionna in horror. "I hadn't had a chance to ask her yet," he croaked out.

"Oh." Brionna's eyes widened, and she put a hand on Charlotte's arm. "I'm so sorry, Your Highness. I thought you knew."

"Clearly that isn't the case." Charlotte's words were clipped, and a dozen emotions danced across her face—shock, confusion, anger. But it was the look of betrayal that cut Adam to the core.

Brionna motioned back and forth between Charlotte and Adam. "Perhaps I should let the two of you discuss this in private."

Adam wanted to strangle Brionna. But of course she didn't know just how much her slip-up might have cost them, because he'd never told her about his history with Charlotte.

"That's probably a good idea," Adam said.

Brionna nodded. "I really hope you'll consider it, Your Highness. We need your help."

"Brionna," Adam said.

"I'm going." She held up her hands, then turned and scurried away.

"Perhaps we should take this into the hallway," Charlotte said. Her hands were curled into fists at her side, which did nothing to bolster Adam's confidence.

"Good idea," Adam muttered.

They weaved their way through the crowd, and out of the corner of his eye he saw Joseph and Karla following them.

Charlotte didn't stop when they were in the hallway, but instead continued on to an alcove before whirling to face him.

"Do you want to explain to me what is happening right now?" she hissed.

Adam ran a hand through his hair. "Char—"

"Don't call me that." She shook her head, sending the dangling diamond earrings she wore bouncing. "What was Brionna talking about?"

The betrayal was flashing in her eyes again, making his heart crack. "It was something she mentioned after Blessing resigned. You would be an excellent director, but I know—"

"I can't believe this." Charlotte ran a hand through her hair, tousling the curls falling softly around her shoulders. "That's why you've been so nice to me—earlier in the suite, and then just now after my speech."

"What? No, I—"

"And Chief Mandla was in on it. Ooo!" Charlotte flung out a hand, nearly hitting him on the shoulder. "You are unbelievable. I can't believe I ever thought I had feelings for you."

Feelings for him? Adam took a step toward Charlotte, his heart suddenly pounding very rapidly in his chest. "Wait. What do you mean, feelings for me?"

She folded her arms tightly, glaring up at him. "You knew how much it would hurt me when you didn't call. Yet you did it anyway. Why?"

He felt his defenses immediately rise, and the guilt followed closely behind. "Communication is a two-way street. I didn't see you pick up the phone, either."

"Why would I, once Brionna entered the picture?"

Brionna. Adam had almost forgotten about her. She was the reason he was in this fight with Charlotte.

Or maybe he needed to stop blaming others and realize this was all on him.

He rubbed a hand over his face, feeling suddenly exhausted. "I should have called."

Charlotte laughed, the sound cutting like blades. "Yet another manipulation tactic. I'm not sure why I'm even surprised anymore. You'll clearly say or do anything to get your way."

"What? I don't even know what you're talking about."

"You've been trying to reel me back in since I got here, and it almost worked." Charlotte brushed at her cheeks, and Adam realized she was crying. "But Emma was right. Well, it's not going to work, Adam Montgomery. I'm finished."

Adam leaned forward, placing a hand on the wall behind her head. He heard her small intake of breath. She pulled her bottom lip between her teeth, hands pressed flat against the wall as she leaned into it, and suddenly Adam's heart was racing for an entirely different reason.

"I wasn't trying to manipulate you," Adam said, his voice low. "Asking you to help with the school was Brionna's idea. But I think it's a good one. You could come back to South Africa after the wedding, and we could work together to get it open. In five seconds, you came up with a brilliant idea no one else has thought of in six months."

Her chest heaved as she stuttered in a breath. Adam let his eyes rove her face, taking in the angles of it. It would be so easy to slip his hand behind her head and cover her lips with his.

"I have responsibilities in Durham," Charlotte whispered.

"I know," Adam said. "But you could travel back and forth as much as you needed to. This is your dream,

Char. I'd give you total control over the project. We'd do things your way, as long as it meant we could still open on time."

"What about Brionna?"

He'd been an idiot to try to stay away from Charlotte. Adam reached out, letting his index finger gently trace the curve of her lips. "She isn't my girlfriend. We've never even been on a date. Lots of business dinners, but no real dates."

"You never called," Charlotte whispered.

"That's because I'm an idiot."

Adam leaned forward, and Charlotte's eyelids fluttered closed.

In that moment, Adam didn't care that his mother wanted him to be with Brionna. He didn't care that merging the two companies would make his father proud. Because Charlotte was right here, and she was his.

Adam let his own eyes close as he leaned down, anticipating the soft brush of her lips. She wore a strawberry-flavored lip gloss that drove him wild, and he couldn't wait to taste it once more.

"No!" Two hands hit his chest, pushing him firmly backward.

Adam stumbled away from Charlotte, stunned. He crashed into a potted plant, sending it flying to the floor with a loud *crash*. His arms pinwheeled wildly as he tried to regain his balance. And then he was falling, his butt landing smack dab in the middle of the spilled soil.

Joseph and Karla were at Charlotte's side in an instant.

"I'm done with you, Adam Montgomery." Charlotte pointed a shaky finger in his direction. "I'm not some . . . some puppet that you can command with a kiss. Find someone else to help you with the school."

She brushed past him, the flared fabric of her skirts whipping him in the face. Joseph and Karla followed after her, not giving Adam a second glance.

Adam carefully extricated himself from the mess, careful not to cut his hands on the broken pieces of pottery. What had just happened?

He brushed at the seat of his pants, knocking loose the dirt that clung there. Thank heaven the plant hadn't been watered recently, and his suit jacket would cover most of the stain. What a night.

Adam made his way back into the ballroom and found an employee. After asking him to make sure the mess in the hallway got cleaned up, Adam searched the room for Brionna.

He didn't have to search for long. She soon found him, an apologetic smile on her thin lips.

"I'm so sorry," she said. "I didn't realize you hadn't talked to her about it yet."

"A heads up would have been nice," Adam said.

Brionna glanced at his pants. "Why is there dirt all over your suit?"

"Long story," Adam muttered. "I'm going to my room. See you tomorrow."

In his suite, Adam tugged his tie loose and flopped onto his bed. Charlotte still had feelings for him. Feelings that he'd apparently reawakened in the past two days.

Never calling her had been a cowardly move, but Adam had convinced himself it was for the best. He and Charlotte had both known it was just a fling, and they lived worlds apart. She was a princess, bound by her duty to the royal family just as he was bound by duty to his. It would never work.

Except when she'd stood so close to him tonight, the vanilla scent of her perfume surrounding him, he'd found himself wondering why it wouldn't work.

"Argh!" Adam grabbed a pillow, burying his face in its soft cushion.

He'd give her space tonight. They both needed time to cool down. But tomorrow, they needed to talk—not only about the school, but about what had really happened in Durham.

Chapter Twelve

Charlotte had almost let Adam kiss her.

She closed her eyes, dizziness overwhelming her as the jeep bounced along the pockmarked dirt road. It had taken Adam less than forty-eight hours to trap her once more in his spell. If Brionna hadn't let his ulterior motives slip, Charlotte might have given her heart over to him once more.

The jeep hit a pothole, sending a jarring *zing* up Charlotte's spine. She grabbed hold of the jeep's side bar to keep from slamming into Emma. The wind whipped long strands of hair against her cheeks, making them sting. She tried to brush the strands back into her ponytail, but the jeep accelerated and the wind played with them once more.

"This is amazing!" Emma threw her hands into the air with a laugh.

Charlotte grimaced, tasting dust. She'd never ridden in an open-air jeep before, and she wasn't sure if she liked the experience.

Adam had told her on one starry night in Durham that if she ever came to South Africa, he'd take her on a safari ride. Now she was here, in South Africa, on that tour he'd spoken so enthusiastically about—without him. Adam had shown his true colors.

Emma grabbed Charlotte's hand, pointing into the distance with a squeal. "I think I see a zebra. Yes, there's a whole pack of them! Or is it called a herd?"

The driver glanced over his shoulder, one hand loosely on the steering wheel. Junior had ebony skin that shone with a sheen of sweat and wore the stereotypical khaki shorts and wide-brimmed hat of a safari tour guide. "A collection of zebras is called a dazzle."

"Wow. How cool is that?" Emma glanced over at Charlotte, her grin faltering. "Aren't you having a good time?"

Charlotte swallowed, forcing a smile. "Of course I am. We're on an African safari—how could I not have fun?"

She hated that she was allowing Adam to ruin this for her.

Joseph shifted in the passenger seat, his expression unreadable as usual. The rest of the security detail rode in the jeep behind them—their own private tour of the savanna. In the twenty minutes since they'd left the hotel, they'd already seen a herd of gazelles and a hawk gliding effortlessly through the cloudless blue sky.

Charlotte watched as the zebras darted gracefully through the tall yellow grasses. They seemed so free of life's burdens, their only concern when they'd eat next. It must be nice.

"Those zebras are too far away to see very well," Junior said. "We'll try to find a dazzle closer to the road so we can really appreciate them."

"Excellent," Emma said.

Five minutes later, the jeep began to slow. Junior brought the jeep to a crawl, the hum of the engine suddenly loud in the stillness of nature.

"Look over there," he said, keeping his voice low as he pointed to a cluster of trees about fifty yards off the road. "Do you see them?"

Charlotte squinted, then gasped when she realized lions were lounging beneath those trees. She grabbed the binoculars hanging around her neck and brought them to her eyes. One male lion sat in the middle of the pride. A full mane of shaggy brown hair surrounded his face, and his dark eyes seemed to stare right at Charlotte. Three females lay beside him, along with a cub.

"Incredible," Emma breathed. "Can we get closer?"

"No," Joseph said shortly.

Charlotte rolled her eyes and lowered her binoculars. "You're no fun."

"My job has no place for fun," Joseph said.

Emma smirked. "Just remember that you said it, not us."

"It wouldn't be safe to get much closer than this to the animals, anyway," Junior said. "If they choose to come closer to the road, that's okay, but we shouldn't venture into their territory." He put the car back in gear and slowly pressed on the gas, easing away from the lions. "There is a watering hole about a mile from here that's very popular with the animals. If we're lucky, we'll see some elephants and giraffes there, maybe even a hippo or two. Then we'll head toward the river. Usually you can see a few crocodiles in there."

"Perfect," Charlotte said.

Adam had told her once that the elephants were his favorite animal. He'd teased her more than once about riding one together.

The lions were far in the distance now, and the jeep picked up speed once more. Charlotte gave up trying to brush the hair out of her face. She'd just have to deal with the rat's nest when she got back to the Hotel Montgomery. She was already thinking of excuses to spend the next day and a half in her room so she wouldn't have to run into Adam. Hopefully, he'd be so busy trying to find a new school director that he wouldn't have time to hang around the hotel lobby, waiting to ambush her.

But what if he couldn't find a new director? If the tribe decided to sue the hotel, the project would come to a grinding halt and probably never be finished.

She hated Adam for dangling her dream in front of her, only to reveal himself as a fraud. Helping open the school would have been some version of heaven. But not under these circumstances. Not when Adam had used her emotions against her to try to trick her into doing his bidding.

Emma squeezed Charlotte's hand, bringing her back to the present. Emma's eyes were dark with concern, her lips turned up in a sympathetic smile. After pushing Adam into that plant last night, Charlotte had told Emma everything—about how he wanted her to be the director of the school, about how Charlotte had freaked out, about the almost-kiss.

"I've been thinking," Emma said, her voice light. "Now that you've given your keynote address, do we really need to stay for the rest of the conference? I talked to Becky this morning, and she said that we haven't committed to anything else."

"True," Charlotte said slowly. "I guess there really is no reason to stick around here then."

"I only mention it because I found this fabulous spa in the city that I'm dying to try out before we go back to Durham," Emma said. "I am dying for a hot stone massage, and there's this adorable little library in a really historic building that I thought maybe you'd enjoy."

That did catch Charlotte's interest. "A library?"

Emma nodded. "Would you mind terribly if we headed into the city today? We could leave right after the safari and have all of tomorrow to spend there, and we'd be that much closer to the airport to fly home. I'm sure Becky could find us a hotel, even on this short of notice."

Charlotte's heart swelled with gratitude, and she gave Emma a quick hug. She knew that while Emma would enjoy the spa, she really didn't care if they went or not. But Emma knew how painful it would be for Charlotte to see Adam again, and she was giving her an easy out.

"Yes, I suppose that would be fine," Charlotte said, her voice thick with tears. "It would be a pity to come all this way and not at least visit the library. I'll send Becky a text right now and have her book us a hotel. Will that be enough time for you to check out the place, Joseph?"

No doubt Joseph would throw a fit over the change of plans—he hated anything that posed a security threat, however slight, and in his mind changing hotels would definitely fall into that category. But

Joseph just nodded and said, "As soon as Becky gives us the hotel name, we'll look into things."

Affection for Joseph had Charlotte blinking back tears, and she was suddenly so grateful for these people in her life who cared about her.

"It's a deal, then," Emma said. "Tell Becky to have the staff start packing our things."

Charlotte nodded and sent a quick text, then set her phone back in her lap. Suddenly the wind felt warm and comforting, and she was eager to get to the watering hole and hopefully check a few more African animals off her bucket list before they left this place forever.

As though the driver had read her mind, the jeep started to slow down, and Charlotte saw the watering hole up ahead.

Suddenly a hippopotamus rose from the depths of the pool, its ears wiggling and mouth open wide, tongue lolling out of the side.

Resolve flowed through Charlotte. Adam had stolen enough from her. She wouldn't allow him to steal the joy of this once-in-a-lifetime experience as well. She had somewhere around forty hours left to spend in South Africa, and she was going to enjoy every one of them.

Chapter Thirteen

$\mathscr{B}$rionna burst into Adam's office, her face flushed and eyes wide. "They're gone."

Adam glanced at Keith, who lifted a shoulder in a shrug. They'd just been discussing the new security guards, who were to arrive later that afternoon. Adam had high hopes that it would end the issues with vandalism, even though he hated that the suggestion had been Brionna's. He wasn't sure why that bothered him so much and figured it was better not to analyze the situation.

"What are you talking about?" Adam asked Brionna. Didn't she know how to knock? "Who's gone?"

"I can't believe you don't know." Brionna put a hand to her forehead, chest heaving. "This is your hotel. You should already be aware of this."

Adam rose, frustration making his words come out harsher than he'd intended. He hadn't asked for her opinion on how he ran the Hotel Montgomery, but lately it seemed that was all she gave. "Why don't you tell me what's going on, and maybe I can fix it?"

"There's no fixing this," Brionna said. "Princess Charlotte and Princess Emma left the hotel about an hour ago."

Adam's heart lurched, but he reminded himself that they were on a safari tour with Junior. Adam had woken up that morning, desperate to find Charlotte and apologize to her. After failing to locate her in the dining room or in any of the classrooms where the conference was taking place, he'd asked the front desk if they had any ideas and learned the princesses were out. "Yes, I know. But they'll be back in a few hours."

Brionna pushed a hand through her hair, her stance still tense. "You don't understand. They've checked out of their suite. I don't know if they're heading back to Durham early, or spending the next two nights in the city, but they aren't coming back to the Hotel Montgomery."

Adam's veins suddenly felt flooded with ice. Charlotte was gone? His pulse throbbed in his temples. She wasn't supposed to leave until the day after tomorrow. He was supposed to be able to track her down tonight, if she didn't make an appearance in the dining room for dinner, and apologize.

He turned to Keith, hoping his expression was calm. "I think we're about done here. Let me know how it goes with the new security guards."

"Sure thing, boss. We'll talk more later." Keith scurried away, shooting Brionna a curious glance before shutting the office door behind him.

Brionna collapsed into the chair that Keith had just vacated, shaking her head in disgust. "This is a disaster. How are we supposed to convince Charlotte to be the director of the school if she isn't here?"

Adam folded his arm, his defenses rising more and more with every word. If Brionna hadn't mentioned the school to Charlotte, she'd probably still be here. Instead, she was gone.

Gone. Adam pressed the heels of his hands into his eyes, the implication finally hitting him. There would be no talking to her in the dining room tonight. No apologizing.

No reconciliation.

He'd royally screwed up this time. And yes, he needed Charlotte's help with the school, but this was about more than that. The accusations she'd hurled at him hurt, and he hated that she believed they were true.

"We need Princess Charlotte if we're going to have so much as a prayer of opening the school on time," Brionna said. "Last night I went through all of the applications submitted at the same time as Blessing's.

The options are beyond slim. I checked with human resources, and that position was open for more than three months before Blessing was finally hired. We don't have three months, Adam. We don't have three weeks. At this point, I'm not even sure we have three days."

The reality of the situation hit him. He had a school that was woefully behind schedule, a school director that had just quit, and vandals that he couldn't catch intent on the school's total destruction. And now Charlotte—the woman he was beginning to think he might actually love—was gone.

Their time together had been so short. Had he really fallen in love with her in only ten days?

He never should have let Charlotte go. That almost-kiss last night had been much more than the heightened emotions of the moment.

"You're going to fix this, right?" Brionna said. "We need her. Whatever you said that upset her last night, you have to take it back."

"I know," Adam said. But how could he possibly fix this? He couldn't drop everything and fly to Durham.

Unless he could.

An idea began to form in Adam's mind. One just crazy enough that it might work.

"Don't worry," Adam told Brionna. "I'm on it. I'll see if I can't mend things with Her Highness."

He had to get Charlotte to come back to South Africa. Maybe, if they worked together on the school, she'd see that he wasn't a bad guy.

He had to win back the princess.

"Good." Brionna rose. "I know the timing is horrible, but I have to go check out those properties near Cape Town. I won't be back for at least a week—maybe longer if we finally settle on something to buy."

"No problem," Adam said. He'd have to word things just right with Charlotte. Her accusations of manipulating her emotions made him over-think every word. "Have a safe trip."

Brionna folded her arms, cocking her head to one side as she stared at him. "Are you sure you'll be okay while I'm gone?"

The question made Adam bristle. He'd been manager of this resort long before Brionna arrived, and he hadn't asked for her help on anything since she'd gotten here. How had she infiltrated so much of his life without him even realizing it? "Yeah, I think I can handle it."

"Okay." Brionna hesitated, then leaned across the desk and dropped a swift kiss on Adam's cheek. "I'll see you in a few days then."

Adam put a hand to his cheek. The kiss had been so brief that he almost wondered if he'd imagined it. "See you," he said.

Brionna gave him a shy smile, then slipped out of the room.

What had that been for? Adam leaned back in his chair, Brionna's odd behavior confusing him. They'd never been physically affectionate with each other.

The events of the past few minutes had sapped all his energy, and he felt completely drained. But he couldn't think about Brionna right now. He had to fix things with Charlotte.

Adam grabbed his cell phone and brought up his father's phone number. A moment later, the line clicked on.

"Adam," Father said. "I'm heading into a meeting. Can't this wait?"

"No. I promise it will just take a moment," Adam said quickly. "Did you ever accept the invitation to the royal wedding?"

It would be the perfect excuse to see Charlotte again. Maybe, if they were surrounded by happy guests and the euphoria of the wedding, she'd be willing to listen to his apology.

"Prince Alexander's wedding?" Father asked. "Yes, of course. I accepted the invitation months ago. The timing is extremely inconvenient, but if we don't make an appearance, I'm worried that it will reflect badly on Montgomery Hotels & Resorts. There are some tax breaks I'm hoping to push through in the next parliamentary session and attending the wedding will garner us some goodwill."

Hope sprang to life in Adam's chest. "Would you mind if I attended the wedding with you? Assuming you got a plus one, of course." No way his father would take a date—not so soon after Mother's death. Adam's heart twinged, and he swallowed hard.

His mother would have loved to attend the royal wedding. Would have enjoyed every moment of the festivities.

Silence stretched across the line, then his father asked cautiously, "You want to go to the royal wedding?"

"If at all possible," Adam said.

"This is perfect!"

Adam yanked the phone away from his ear, surprised by his father's volume.

"By all means take my spot," his father continued. "I've got so much to do, and I had no idea how I was going to fit that blasted wedding into my schedule. I think your presence will be as good as mine, though. I'll have my secretary send you all the details. Thanks for taking care of this, son."

Well, that had been easy. "I'll look for the email," Adam said.

"I've got to go—the meeting's about to start. We'll talk more later." His father hung up without waiting for a response.

Adam set his cell phone back on the desk. It hadn't escaped his notice that his father had used this as an excuse to bow out of the wedding instead of accepting it as an opportunity for the two of them to spend time together. But Adam had his chance to speak to Charlotte again.

And this time, he wasn't going to waste it.

Chapter Fourteen

Adam didn't call. Not that Charlotte had expected him to after how things had ended last time.

But just in case she was wrong, she kept her phone nearby during the hot stone massage, in her purse as she toured the magnificent library, and clutched in her hand during the plane ride back to Durham.

Her phone stayed silent, mocking her for being stupid enough to hope that Adam would apologize.

Charlotte threw herself into the last-minute wedding preparations. Alex's fiancée, Libby, didn't get along well with her future mother-in-law—Mother's nose still wrinkled every time someone mentioned that an American commoner would one day be queen—and Charlotte made it her personal duty as a wedding attendant to keep the peace between the two women.

But thoughts of Adam kept intruding, and the ragged edges of Charlotte's heart ached. Watching her brothers share longing glances and stolen kisses with their fiancées only made things worse.

She was happy for Alex and Stefan. Really. And she was excited to welcome Libby and Jenna to the family. But seeing them so happy only made Charlotte wonder what was wrong with her. How had she allowed herself to fall in love with such a jerk?

Sometimes, the loneliness took her breath away.

On the day of the wedding, Charlotte awoke before dawn to transform her appearance into something photo-perfect. Her stomach quivered with nerves as a team of stylists made sure her hair and makeup were flawless. Meeting the press always made Charlotte feel equal parts nauseous and paralyzed. No doubt they'd be out in spades today to celebrate the union of the crown prince of Durham and his American beauty. Every major news network in the world, and quite a few not-so-major ones, had sent journalists to cover the event.

Charlotte slipped into her lavender wedding attendant dress—Libby kept using the American term *bridesmaid*. The lace sleeves fell just off the shoulders, while the chiffon skirt flowed about her legs. A jeweled applique belt pulled the entire outfit together, and Charlotte had to admit that Libby had good taste. The dress was a perfect blend of Libby's carefree upbringing and Alex's more formal heritage.

The palace stylist declared Charlotte camera ready, and she headed downstairs to the waiting cars. She blinked against the blindingly bright sunlight, taking in the crystal blue sky. It made her miss South Africa with a fierce intensity.

She hoped Little Miss Perfect would find a director for the school soon. Charlotte would never forgive herself if the school failed to open. If that happened, she'd always wonder if her help could have made the difference.

The family's private drive was crowded with conservative black town cars waiting for their occupants. Henry and Oliver already waited beside one of the vehicles, looking dashing in their military dress uniforms. Stefan would serve as best man for Alex today and had no doubt left the palace hours earlier.

Henry hurried forward and extended an arm toward Charlotte. "Ready for today?" he asked.

Charlotte's stomach churned, and she took a slow, steadying breath. "As ready as I ever am for a day spent in front of the cameras."

Henry patted her hand. "No one will even pay attention to you today. All eyes will be on Libby and Alex."

Charlotte rolled her eyes. "That's what you think. Do you have any idea how closely the appearances of the wedding attendants were scrutinized at our dear cousin Nicholas's wedding?"

"That was months ago," Henry said breezily. "Besides, you know how Galians are about fashion."

"I'm not buying it. But thanks for trying to make me feel better."

Emma arrived a few minutes later, and they headed to the cathedral. The streets were crowded with people eager to wish Alex and Libby congratulations on their special day, which made the drive slow. No doubt the spectators were hoping to catch a glimpse of the bride and groom after the ceremony as they made their traditional procession to the palace.

"I can't believe Alex is getting married," Charlotte said, watching the crowds of people as they drove past.

"I can't believe it, either." Emma let out a happy sigh. "Libby is so great. She and Alex really are perfect for each other. Who would have thought their fake engagement would turn into a real one?"

"It's crazy," Charlotte agreed. Alex and Libby's relationship had originally begun as a ruse to fool the press after an actress Alex had dated created quite a scandal based on false stories. Alex had been so broken, and Charlotte had wondered if he'd ever recover. But Libby had somehow crashed through Alex's walls and stolen his heart.

When Charlotte had met Adam, she'd fantasized that maybe one day their story would have a similar happy ending. But she'd only been fooling herself.

The church was a gorgeous Gothic cathedral. Stained-glass windows sparkled like jewels underneath the unusually sunny Durham sky. Even nature was celebrating Alex and Libby's marriage.

Someone opened the car door, and Emma gave Charlotte an excited smile.

"Show time," she said.

Charlotte pressed a hand to her trembling stomach. She was suddenly glad she hadn't had time for breakfast.

The crowd seemed much louder outside of the safety of the car. But Charlotte put on her best princess smile and waved to the crowds.

Libby arrived, looking stunning in her own lace dress and cathedral length veil. Charlotte fussed with Libby's veil and made sure her bouquet of white roses and lilies looked perfect, all the while aware of the cameras flashing nonstop. What would the papers say tomorrow about how Charlotte had handled her wedding attendant duties? Her hands felt clammy and her stomach churned, but she put on a smile and focused on Libby.

Libby positively glowed with happiness. She looked every bit the future queen as she walked confidently up the cathedral stairs. Charlotte followed right behind, along with Emma and Connie, the other attendants.

The aisle seemed to go on forever, but Libby barely seemed to notice. Charlotte focused on keeping her breathing even and steady as soft choir music filled the building. The cathedral was filled with hundreds of guests, but Charlotte reminded herself they were all watching Libby, not her.

Alex looked dashing in his red military dress uniform. His eyes were soft and warm, laser-focused on Libby. Charlotte took her place beside her mother in the front row of the nave, and Emma slid in right beside her.

The priest began the ceremony, but Charlotte barely heard the words. Instead, she focused on Libby and Alex. The love in their eyes was unmistakable, and Charlotte's heart began aching afresh. They stared at each other the entire ceremony, caught in some sort of love bubble that seemed to keep out the world.

Charlotte had felt that bubble during those ten days she and Adam had been together. But the bubble had decidedly burst.

Maybe she should have accepted Brionna's— Adam's?—offer of interim director of the school. Yes, he'd tricked her. But opening a school was still Charlotte's dream. It had been right there, finally within reach, and she'd turned it down because of—what? Pride?

The children shouldn't have to suffer because Charlotte was apparently horrible at relationships.

The priest pronounced Alex and Libby as husband and wife. Charlotte blinked back tears and noticed her mother and Emma doing the same. The newlyweds made their way out of the chapel, the soft choir music accompanying their first steps as a married couple.

And just like that, the family dynamic had been forever altered. Charlotte couldn't be happier for the couple.

Emma exited the row, and Charlotte followed for the formal procession from the church back to the palace. Hundreds of eyes followed her every step. Charlotte tried not to let her fear show, stepping purposefully to appear confident, just as Mrs. Grant had taught her. Men in three-piece suits and women in elaborate fascinators watched her progress down the aisle that seemed to go on forever.

She was finally to the back of the chapel. Charlotte could see the outer room just beyond, also filled with people, and in the distance the open doors of the cathedral. Alex and Libby had nearly made it outside. Charlotte smiled at the crowd, willing herself not to walk too quickly.

In the endless sea of people, a familiar face smiled back.

Charlotte quickly looked forward again, willing herself not to run from the chapel. She had to be imagining things. Yes, he came from nobility and had doubtlessly received an invitation. But if he was coming to the wedding, why hadn't he mentioned it?

Maybe her mind was playing tricks on her. She sneaked another glance at the crowd, quickly locating the familiar strong jaw and blue eyes.

It was no mistake. Adam was back in Durham.

Chapter Fifteen

Charlotte felt dizzy, like she'd gone around one too many times on a carousel. She blinked rapidly, trying to erase the black spots from her vision. The choir music seemed too loud, the aisle too long.

Why was Adam here? Better yet, why hadn't he mentioned he was coming?

She focused on putting one foot in front of the other and maintaining her princess smile. No doubt her surprise and disbelief at seeing Adam here had been written all over her face. Hopefully, no cameras had caught the moment. Maggie, the palace press secretary, would be furious if that became front-page news instead of Alex and Libby's traditional balcony kiss.

Outside, Charlotte quickly climbed into one of the waiting sedans. Emma slid onto the seat right after her, and soon they were making the slow drive back to the palace.

Emma smoothed back her dark hair, raising one eyebrow. "What happened in there? You froze in the middle of the aisle, then started walking a little too fast."

Charlotte winced. Her palms were clammy, but she didn't want to wrinkle her chiffon skirt by rubbing them on it. "Was it that noticeable?"

"Only to me," Emma said. Charlotte breathed a little easier—Emma always told the truth, even when it hurt. "I don't think anyone else was paying close enough attention to catch the shift. What's wrong?"

Everything was wrong, and Charlotte had no idea how to make things right again. She wished she had a book to hold right now. The comforting weight of a novel would go a long way toward soothing her nerves. "Did you know Adam was coming to the wedding?"

Emma's eyes widened. "Adam. As in, Adam Montgomery?"

Charlotte nodded. "I saw him near the back of the chapel."

"Wow." Emma rested her head against the soft leather seat of the sedan. "I had no idea he was coming. He really never mentioned anything about the wedding to you?"

Charlotte raised her eyebrow in what she hoped was an *are you serious?* glare. "I'm pretty sure I wouldn't forget that important of a detail."

Emma nodded. "Good point."

The car was nearly halfway back to the palace now. The crowds of celebrating people lining the streets had only grown thicker, their enthusiastic cheers floating through the car's thick bulletproof windows. But all Charlotte could think about was Adam Montgomery. Why had he come back to Durham? It couldn't only be about the wedding, or he would have mentioned it to her. Right?

"I didn't see his father," Charlotte said. "Maybe he's here as the earl's proxy for today."

Emma nodded slowly. "I guess that would make sense. It's expected that at least one member of each noble family will attend, and if something came up for Lord Nottingshire, he might have asked Adam to come in his place."

"That's probably it then." No doubt the earl was an extremely busy man. Any number of things could have prevented him from attending.

Except that Adam was already severely behind schedule on the school. He didn't have time to fly to another continent and watch two strangers say *I do*. Not unless his trip served a dual purpose.

Like persuading Charlotte to become the interim director for his school.

For the first time since Brionna's slip of the tongue, Charlotte wondered what the harm would be in accepting the offer. There was nothing pressing for her in Durham, and Adam had said she could go back and forth between the two countries as often as needed.

"Char?"

She blinked, bringing Emma's concerned face back into focus. "Sorry. Did you say something?"

"I asked if you're going to talk to Adam. He'll probably be at the second reception. His father's rank is high enough that he might even be at the first."

"If he comes up to me, I can't exactly create a scene. Nothing should steal the focus from Alex and Libby."

Now Emma's voice was tinged with panic. "You aren't considering going back to South Africa, are you?"

"Would it be so awful if I did?" Charlotte held out her hands pleadingly to Emma. "This is the opportunity of a lifetime. You know how hard I've tried to convince Mother to let me start a similar project in Durham. Maybe if I can show her I was successful in South Africa, she'll reconsider."

"But you'd be spending all day, every day with Adam."

"He won't burn me a third time," Charlotte said, her tone resolute. "I won't let him. Besides, he probably spends most of his day occupied by hotel business, not the school. Why else would he need a director?"

"You're not thinking clearly. The school doesn't open for another three and a half months. That's an eternity."

"It's hardly any time at all," Charlotte countered. "I don't even know if that's why Adam is here. Maybe he'll completely avoid me at the receptions."

"You're playing with fire, Char. Be careful."

As soon as they entered the palace, a stylist pulled Charlotte and Emma into a room for touch-ups, then Charlotte posed for what felt like hours while the official wedding photographs were taken before being ushered into the ballroom for the first reception. There would be four in total before the night was over, and Charlotte was required to attend them all.

Charlotte entered the room cautiously. The reception—this one specifically for the closest friends and family of the bride and groom, along with the upper nobility of Durham—was already in full swing. A string quartet played on a raised stage in one corner of the ballroom. Men in suits and women wearing elegant dresses laughed and talked, while waiters in tuxedos circles the room with their trays of food and drink.

She scanned the room, heart in her throat as she looked for signs of Adam.

"Would you care for a drink, Your Highness?"

Charlotte put a hand to her chest, trying to still the frantic beating of her heart. She gave the waiter what she hoped was a gracious smile and accepted the glass of a champagne with a murmured, "Thank you."

She didn't usually drink, but Charlotte took one careful sip to calm her nerves. Adam wasn't a giant or anything, but he was usually one of the tallest people in a room and easy to pick out of a crowd.

Many of the women still wore their fascinators from the wedding, making it harder to comb through the crowd for Adam. Charlotte caught the eye of her cousin, Nicholas, and his bride of only a few months, Kara. The two were a handsome couple. Kara had the lithe body of a dancer, beautiful brown hair that hung about her shoulders in loose curls, and blue eyes that instantly made Charlotte think of Adam. Nicholas was her perfect opposite, with his wavy blond hair, green eyes, and tanned skin.

Kara tugged on her husband's hand, heading toward Charlotte.

"How are you?" she asked in French, giving Charlotte a big hug.

Charlotte switched to French—Kara was just learning English and still struggled with the unfamiliar language—and put on her best smile. "Fantastic, of course. How is married life treating the two of you?"

Kara wrapped an arm around Nicholas's waist, leaning into him. She gazed up at her husband with eyes dewy with love. "Being at the palace has been a bit of an adjustment, but I have no complaints."

Nicholas chuckled, dropping a kiss on the crown of Kara's head. "Imagine that. You know, most women would love to live in a palace."

Kara crinkled her nose and said in a teasing tone, "Yes, well, I'm not most people."

"And I couldn't be more grateful for that."

"You two are nauseatingly adorable," Charlotte said.

Kara and Nicholas had met in large part because of Alex. After the scandal broke in the press with Isla, Alex had escaped to Galia to hide from the media. Nicholas's attempts to help Alex had ended in them accidentally breaking into Kara's dance studio. And the rest was history.

"Did you bring Esmée with you?" Charlotte asked. She was Kara's two-year-old niece, who she'd adopted after her sister died of a drug overdose. "I would love to see her."

"Nicholas convinced me to leave her in Galia with her nanny," Kara said. "She's so busy these days and would have spent the whole time in our room with the nanny, anyway."

"I guess I'll just have to try to squeeze in a visit soon, then," Charlotte said.

"I'd love that," Kara said, her eyes brightening. "Sometime soon for sure."

Someone cleared their throat behind her, and Charlotte's entire body instantly went clammy with sweat. She turned slowly, but she already knew who she'd see.

Adam.

He looked regal in a navy three-piece suit, his beard neatly trimmed and eyes full of an emotion she couldn't quite name.

"Your Highness," he said, bowing from the waist. His French was nearly perfect, with only the barest hint of a Durham accent coloring the vowels.

She'd never heard Adam speak French before. And she liked it more than she should.

"Adam Montgomery." Nicholas grabbed Adam's hand in a shake, and the two men clapped each other on the back. "It's so good to see you. How's that South African project going?"

"Excellent," Adam said. "In fact, Charlotte and Emma were just there for an education conference. You really should come down sometime. I'll take you on a safari."

"Sounds fantastic," Nicholas said. "Have you met my wife, Kara?"

"Only very briefly at your wedding," Adam said as the two shook hands. "A pleasure, Your Highness."

Kara's cheeks blushed scarlet. "Please, call me Kara. I'm still trying to get used to the title."

Adam had been at Kara and Nicholas's wedding? Charlotte didn't remember seeing him there. Of course,

162

they hadn't met at that point, and there'd been a lot of people at the wedding and subsequent receptions.

"I'm sorry," Charlotte interrupted. "But how do the two of you know each other?"

Nicholas wrapped an arm around Adam with a grin. "We met at Yale University in Connecticut. As luck would have it, we happened to do our semester abroad at the same school, at the same time. We had some really good times there, didn't we, Adam?"

"The very best," Adam agreed. "Nicholas's flat was just across the hall from mine. I always knew he'd help me out if I was in a pinch."

"Not that you needed it," Nicholas countered.

"I'm so glad to have finally met you." Kara offered an apologetic smile. "Perhaps we can talk more later. Right now, I'm afraid it's nearly Esmée's bedtime. If you'll excuse me, I want to call and wish her good night."

"I'll go with you." Nicholas placed a hand at the small of Kara's back. "Adam, let's catch up soon."

"In South Africa," Adam said, pointing a finger at Nicholas. "I'm holding you to that promise. You'll love the resort."

"Definitely," Nicholas said. "We'll talk more later."

Kara and Nicholas were leaving her alone with Adam? Panic flared in Charlotte's chest, and she wanted to yell after the couple, *Come back!*

But they didn't get her telepathic message. Despite the crowds of people pressing in around them, Charlotte was suddenly very much alone with Adam Montgomery.

She reluctantly looked up at him, her stomach quivering. The high energy of the ballroom had already exhausted Charlotte, and this encounter with Adam wasn't helping. She could feel herself pulling inward, her energy drained.

"You didn't say goodbye," Adam said finally.

"I didn't feel I owed you that, considering the circumstances." It was hard to keep her tone friendly, in case any of the nearby guests were eavesdropping on the conversation. "I didn't realize you were coming to the wedding. Seems like it would have come up during one of our conversations in South Africa."

"When I realized you'd left, I called my father and begged him to let me attend the wedding in his place. I had to see you again, Char."

Charlotte quickly glanced around, then took a step closer to Adam. "You shouldn't address me so familiarly. Not here."

Excited whoops and enthusiastic clapping filled the ballroom then, making Charlotte flinch at the sudden rise in noise. Libby and Alex had just entered the room, claiming everyone's undivided attention.

Everyone but Adam's.

"I swear on my mother's grave, I wasn't trying to manipulate you," Adam said, his lips just brushing Charlotte's ear.

She shivered, turning back around to face him and taking a few steps back. She needed to put some distance between them. Needed to clear her head.

"You shouldn't swear on people's graves," she said, putting a hand to her forehead.

"Normally I would never so much as consider it." He reached out, taking her hand and cupping it in both of his. "That's how important it is to me that you believe what I'm telling you. I am so sorry if you felt that my feelings for you were anything less than genuine."

His hands were warm and soft on hers, and she could feel her heart thawing at the honesty in his eyes.

But she couldn't let herself make the same mistake a third time. Reluctantly, she pulled her hand away.

Alex held a champagne glass now and was saying something to the crowd.

Adam made a good show of pretending to pay attention to the toast. Charlotte kept her attention forward, but whispered to Adam, "Would you ever have told me about the interim director position?"

"If you're asking me if the offer was genuine, then my answer is yes. Your expertise would be invaluable on this project. But I know how busy you are, and with our history I wanted to make sure I phrased the offer in exactly the right way."

A way that made it clear he wanted her for the school, not for himself. Charlotte swallowed, her mouth tasting bitter.

"If I did come back," she said slowly, "what would my responsibilities be?"

"You'd basically be a consultant," Adam said quickly. "Blessing was responsible for the hiring of all school staff and overseeing the building's construction, but your knowledge is so much broader than hers. I'd want to utilize that."

Charlotte shook her head, folding her arms. Libby and Alex were sharing a chaste kiss now while the crowd cooed appreciatively.

"Not good enough," Charlotte said. "I want complete control of this. We'd execute the school according to my vision."

Adam didn't even hesitate. "Done. My only stipulations are that we abide by the contract we've signed with the tribe and open by September first."

It would be a tight deadline, but Charlotte knew she could make it work. Her hand started tingling with anticipation.

This was happening. All she had to do was say the word, and she'd be opening a school.

"I want a salary," Charlotte said quickly. "Whatever you were paying Blessing."

Adam raised an eyebrow. "Okay."

"Not for me. I want the sum donated to Education Beyond Borders."

Adam's eyes softened, and he nodded. "Of course. Absolutely."

"My mother will be furious." Polite clapping had filled the room now, Alex and Libby's toast finished.

"Probably," Adam agreed.

Charlotte put her hands to her cheeks. She couldn't believe she was going to agree to this. Wasn't *don't work with your ex* one of the cardinal rules of breakups? "I would have to be free to come and go from Durham as much as necessary."

"You'd have the use of the Montgomery jet whenever you required it. I promise."

Charlotte dropped her hands, unable to stop smiling. She hated that Adam could see how happy this was making her. Hated that her dream was coming to life because of him. "Okay then. I guess I'm going back to South Africa. When do we leave?"

Adam coughed, running a hand over his jaw. "Are you serious?"

Charlotte nodded. "I think I've made my intentions pretty clear."

"Great! This is excellent news." Charlotte glanced at Adam and saw a broad smile on his face. "I was planning to fly home sometime tomorrow, but I can push that back a day or two if that's better for your schedule."

Mother was going to kill her. But Charlotte couldn't give up this opportunity. She couldn't let down the students who would one day attend that school.

"Tomorrow is fine," Charlotte said.

Adam groaned, crushing Charlotte to him in a tight hug. "Thank you," he whispered, the sincerity in his voice unmistakable. "You have no idea what this means to me."

Charlotte squirmed away from him, wary of the crowds. But no one was paying attention to their conversation—all eyes were focused on the bride and groom. "I'm only doing this for the children."

"I'll take what I can get. We'll leave tomorrow then. You pick the time."

I'll take what I can get. What was that supposed to mean? Charlotte threaded her fingers together, pressing her linked hands against her quivering stomach. "Ten o'clock?"

"I'll be ready."

Chapter Sixteen

"I know what you're doing."

Adam glanced over, surprised to see Emma standing beside him. Alex and Libby had just cut the wedding cake, and the first reception was nearly at a close.

"What am I doing?" Adam asked.

He still couldn't believe that Charlotte was coming back to South Africa with him. He'd come into today hoping to apologize. Instead, she'd brought up South Africa and agreed to be the interim director.

The school wouldn't open for more than three months. Surely that would be enough time to prove to Charlotte just how much she meant to him.

"You're trying to make her fall in love with you again," Emma said. Her words were soft and pleasant, but her eyes shot daggers. "I don't think you realize just how much you hurt her the last time. She was devastated when you never called."

"I made a mistake," Adam said. "Now I'm trying to fix it."

"If you care for her at all, you'll leave her alone," Emma said. Then she walked away, not giving him a chance to respond.

Emma's words stayed with Adam all night. He slept fitfully, plagued by bizarre dreams where Charlotte told him that he'd ruined her life, then turned into a yardstick and whacked him over the head. By the time he dragged himself aboard the private jet, he'd nearly convinced himself that he'd imagined yesterday's conversation with Charlotte. Maybe she'd never show up, and he'd have to fly home alone.

But at ten o'clock on the dot, he heard the hum of a car engine on the tarmac.

Adam rose, going to the open plane door in disbelief. A tall, burly man with dark sunglasses—was it Joseph?—held open the door of a black town car.

A long leg emerged, wearing a dark-colored heel. Charlotte's head appeared over the top of the door.

She'd come.

Her face was half-hidden by dark sunglasses, her lips pressed into an unreadable line as she gazed up at the plane. Her blonde hair was pulled back in a loose ponytail, the curls just brushing her shoulders. He still did a double take every time he saw her blonde instead of brunette, but the color suited her somehow. She wore a light blue dress that wrapped around her waist, making it look tiny, then flared at the hips and fell to just below her knees. But it was the small paperback book she clutched in one hand that made his heart start beating wildly.

Adam bounded down the steps, excitement making it hard not to rush.

"You made it," he said.

"Your airstrip wasn't hard to find," Charlotte said.

He ached to pull her into his arms for a hug, but her tone clearly said she wasn't ready for that. So Adam swallowed his feelings and motioned to the stairs. "Well, follow me. I'll show you around."

Charlotte nodded and walked up the steps. Adam followed behind her, resolutely staring down at his feet instead of enjoying the view her ascent provided.

Inside the plane, Charlotte pulled off her sunglasses and perched them on top of her head, looking around the cabin. "Wow. I had no idea that Montgomery Hotels & Resorts was doing so well."

A surprised chuckle escaped Adam, and he quickly put a fist to his mouth. "I imagine the royal family has pretty nice accommodations for private travel."

"We do have a private plane, and I suppose it's adequate," Charlotte said primly. "But often we fly commercial, especially if members of the family need to be in two places at once. First class, but still—not as nice as this."

Adam looked around, trying to see the plane through her eyes. The front held a small living room, with two cream-colored couches with a gray geometric design pattern facing a black coffee table. A television hung on the wall opposite the coffee table so that both couches could see it, and in front of that were four reclining chairs with their own private TV screens. The back half of the plane held a bedroom for those long international flights and a full bathroom, and a galley kitchen allowed for simple meals to be prepared en route.

"Thank you," Adam said. Then, more softly, he added, "My mom remodeled the entire jet just before her cancer diagnosis."

Charlotte's lips softened, her jaw relaxing its tight clench. "She had excellent taste. I love the fabric choices."

Adam looked away, blinking back the moisture suddenly filling his eyes. He didn't want to cry in front of Charlotte. It had been nearly a year since his mother's death, after all. He motioned to the couches. "Please, take a seat. We'll leave just as soon as your luggage is loaded."

"Perfect." Charlotte sank gracefully onto the proffered seat, and Joseph and Karla claimed the reclining seats just behind her. Becky had arrived on the plane now and was directing the driver where to set the luggage. There were a lot of suitcases. Adam took that as a good sign that Charlotte planned to stay in South Africa for a while.

"I thought maybe I could show you the blueprints for the school during the flight," Adam said. "Obviously we can't make structural changes at this point, but I'd love to get your input on the design choices that Blessing made."

"Great," Charlotte said. "I want to hit the ground running when we get to South Africa. Show me what you've got."

Adam nodded and pushed a button underneath the coffee table. A section of it rose, then extended out until it rested just above his lap as a desk.

"Wow," Charlotte said. "How did you do that?"

"Oh." Adam leaned over the coffee table and pushed the button for her own desk.

"So cool," Charlotte said. "I'll have to tell my father about this. It would be really convenient on our plane."

"I can give you the contact information for the company that designed it," Adam said.

Charlotte smiled, nodding enthusiastically. "That would be great."

"I'll text my father for the info as soon as we land."

A shadow crossed Charlotte's features, and she suddenly became cool and distant once more. "You were going to show me the plans?"

"Uh, right." Adam turned his laptop around, showing her the screen. "It's kind of small, but you've already toured the school so you get the idea."

Charlotte nodded, accepting the computer that Becky handed her. "What enrollment numbers are you expecting?"

Right to business. That was okay, though. Adam needed all the help he could get, and Charlotte seemed willing to give it.

The flight attendant sealed the door, and soon the plane was taxiing down the runway. By the time they were airborne, Adam and Charlotte were deep in conversation about the school. The tension between them slipped away, and Charlotte's entire face lightened as they discussed what Blessing had already done for the project, and the difficulties that kept preventing them from moving forward.

Hours slipped by. At some point, Charlotte moved to the seat beside Adam so she could better see his computer screen. The vanilla scent of her perfume mixed with the strawberry of her shampoo, creating an intoxicating aroma that drove Adam mad. He and Charlotte had discussed her educational goals while together in Durham, but they'd never worked together on something. Adam wasn't at all surprised to find her quick-witted and a hard worker.

The captain's voice came over the intercom, letting them know they would start descending soon. Charlotte closed her laptop lid and lowered the desk back into the coffee table while Adam did the same.

"Thank you for coming back with me," Adam said quietly. "I know your family probably wasn't happy about it."

Charlotte winced. "I might have told them about my plans as I was leaving for the airport. They weren't exactly thrilled, but I didn't give them time to argue."

"Well, I appreciate what you're doing. I know I don't deserve your help, but I'm grateful for it." For the first time in a long time, Adam felt hopeful that they'd open the school by September first. Maybe the tribe wouldn't sue them after all.

"I'm doing this for the school's future students," Charlotte said, her voice suddenly tight. "Not for you. I've tried a long time to open a school like this in Durham, and I decided I was being a selfish idiot for refusing to help just because you were involved."

The words were coated in barbs, and each one found its mark and hung on. Adam curled his hands into fists, willing himself not to let the pain show. "Well, thank you all the same."

She nodded. "You and Brionna are doing a good thing with the school."

Brionna. Adam hadn't thought about her once since leaving South Africa. Bitter guilt coated his tongue, but he batted it away. True, his mother had always said he and Brionna would make a good couple. But Mother had never met Charlotte.

Adam leaned forward, resting his arms on his knees as he stared earnestly at Charlotte. She scooted toward the edge of the couch, putting as much distance between them as possible.

"I know how the magazines make it look," he said quietly. "But Brionna and I aren't really—"

Charlotte held up a hand. "I'm not interested in hearing about your love life."

Adam laughed, the sound hollow. "It's not like that with Brionna."

"You don't owe me an explanation. We both knew that what we had was temporary. Just a fling."

He flinched. Hadn't he said as much himself more than once? But this went so much deeper than a fling. At least it did for him. "I know we both agreed to that."

Charlotte nodded. "You and Brionna will be very happy together, I'm sure. The perfect power couple."

"That's what my mother used to say. She always hoped that Brionna and I would get together one day."

"And now you have."

Adam scooted forward until his knees practically touched Charlotte's. "No. That's what I'm trying to tell you, Char. I think Brionna wants more, but my feelings for her are completely platonic. We're just business associates and old friends. I . . . I've never even kissed her."

"I can't do this." Charlotte rose, walking purposefully to the opposite couch and sitting there—a clear sign she wanted distance from him. "And if this is going to work out—if you really want my help with the school—then you have to let it go. We had a whirlwind romance, and now we don't. There's nothing more to say on the matter."

"But I don't want that," Adam said. "We were good together, Char."

"Then we want different things. I'll help you with the school, Adam. But I can't give you anything more."

The airplane dipped toward the ground, making Adam's stomach swoop with it. He fought back the despair pressing against him, refusing to give in to it.

"I'm not giving up," he said quietly. "You're worth fighting for. And that's exactly what I intend to do."

He'd given Charlotte a million reasons to doubt him. He could only hope that over the next three months, he could give her a million more reasons to trust that his feelings for her were real.

Chapter Seventeen

*E*ntering the presidential suite at the Hotel Montgomery felt like coming home. Charlotte stepped onto the balcony where she and Emma had enjoyed the hot tub and leaned against the railing. She already missed Emma, and it felt a little strange to be in this suite without her. But Charlotte knew she had made the right decision, despite what Emma believed.

Her parents had been less than thrilled when Charlotte announced her plans to return. She'd waited to inform them of her plans until her bags were packed and the car was waiting to take her to the airstrip. And yes, what she'd told them was true—she hadn't wanted to overshadow Alex and Libby's wedding day with her own news—but she'd also selfishly wanted to avoid a confrontation.

Charlotte needed to help open this school, for reasons she didn't fully understand and couldn't explain. And given enough time, her family would have demanded an explanation.

She inhaled deeply, breathing in the dry South African air. The sky was that cheerful blue she loved, and fluffy white clouds floated lazily across it. A giraffe munched leaves from a marula tree only a stone's-throw away, and the school stood proud and strong in the distance.

She'd missed South Africa. Somehow, in those three days she's spent here, the country had imprinted itself on her heart.

Charlotte slept deeply that night and awoke feeling refreshed and eager to jump right into work. She dressed in a simple navy blue skirt and white blouse, then slipped into her most comfortable shoes—the blue pumps with the short heel and insoles.

Her phone buzzed, and she opened the text from Emma. **How's South Africa?**

Great, Charlotte texted back. **I've got a full day of work planned.** Or, more accurately, Becky had it planned. Adam had requested an eight-thirty breakfast meeting, and since Becky still didn't know that Charlotte wanted to avoid Adam as much as possible, the secretary had put it on the schedule.

I hope you know what you're doing.

Charlotte angrily swiped away the text without replying. She was suddenly missing Emma a lot less.

Becky wandered into the room, her tablet in hand. "Five minutes until your eight-thirty breakfast meeting, Your Highness."

"I'm ready," Charlotte said.

"Very good. Breakfast in Mr. Montgomery's suite should end promptly at nine-forty-five, then—"

"Excuse me," Charlotte interrupted. "Did you say in his suite?"

Becky pushed her glasses up the bridge of her nose and nodded. "Yes, his private chef will be serving you there. Is that a problem?"

Charlotte took a deep breath, giving herself one last glance in the mirror. She'd better get used to spending time with Adam. "No, that will be fine. What's the room number?"

It wasn't like she'd be totally alone with Adam. Joseph and Karla would be there.

"Twelve-nineteen," Becky said.

"But that's on this floor." Was it hot in here? Charlotte suddenly felt like her face was burning up.

"Yes." Becky frowned. "Is everything okay, Your Highness?"

No. Adam's room was a mere three doors down from Charlotte's. And she was heading there now for breakfast.

"Everything is fine," Charlotte said. "I guess I'd better get going." She swiped *Pride and Prejudice* from her bedside table on her way out. Suddenly, she couldn't stand the thought of leaving it behind.

The walk to Adam's room was over way too quickly. Charlotte knocked before she could overthink it, steeling herself for an hour spent with Adam.

But it wasn't Adam who opened the door. Brionna, looking plastic and proper, smiled widely at Charlotte and motioned her inside. "Your Highness. It's so good to see you again. Please, come in."

"Oh." Charlotte clutched the book tightly to her chest. She hadn't realized that Brionna would be part of this meeting. "Thank you."

Brionna led Charlotte into the living room, which had the same furniture that was in Charlotte's presidential suite. The suite also had the exact same floor plan, only flipped so that it was a mirror image of hers and with the addition of a full kitchen.

"Adam had to take a phone call," Brionna said, "but he'll be back at any moment. Please, take a seat."

She motioned to the dining room table, which was set for three. Steam billowed from the stove where a man in a chef's coat sautéd something that smelled divine.

Charlotte sat on the edge of one chair. Was she supposed to make small talk with Little Miss Perfect until Adam returned?

182

Brionna sat down at the head of the table, leaving the spot across from Charlotte for Adam.

"We really can't thank you enough for helping us out with the school," Brionna said. "Things have been so stressful lately with all the vandalism. I know that Blessing tried her best, but she really cracked under the pressure."

Charlotte gave Brionna a half-smile. What was she supposed to say to that—*I'm so glad you chose me to become the next stressed-out basket case?*

What did Adam see in Brionna? But it was probably better not to go down that rabbit hole.

"How long have you been helping Adam with the school?" Charlotte asked.

"Pretty much since I got here. That was, oh, maybe seven weeks ago now? Wow. Time really flies when you're having fun." Brionna grabbed the steaming coffee pot and poured Charlotte a cup without asking. "I could see that Adam was in a little over his head, and I was more than happy to lend a helping hand."

Over his head? Charlotte took a sip of her coffee, hoping her skepticism wasn't evident. Adam was a lot of things, but incompetent wasn't one of them. He didn't need Brionna's help. Which must mean she was still here because Adam had feelings for her, whatever he'd claimed yesterday on the plane.

That was okay. Charlotte was only here because of the school.

Adam strode into the room, dropping into the chair across from Charlotte. "Sorry about the wait," he said. "Thanks so much for coming, Char."

Brionna's eyebrow raised at the nickname, and Charlotte quickly took another slow sip of coffee.

"I was just telling Her Highness how grateful we are for the help." Brionna reached across the table, resting her hand on top of Adam's and giving it a squeeze.

Charlotte's heart twinged, and she looked away. Adam said they weren't dating—had never even kissed. But Brionna's actions said otherwise.

The chef set a plate in front of Charlotte and she inhaled deeply. The omelet sizzled on her plate, the cheese melting into the cubed ham.

"Bon appétit," the chef said.

"Thank you, André," Adam said. He gave Charlotte a soft smile. "I hope you like omelets."

He'd made her an omelet for breakfast one morning. She'd been on her way to the Castlebridge Library to read to the children, but first sneaked over to his hotel for a morning kiss. She'd told him it was the most delicious breakfast she'd ever enjoyed.

"It looks delicious," Charlotte said.

"André is the best." Brionna took a bite of her own omelet and moaned. "Delicious."

Charlotte quickly looked down at her plate to hide a laugh.

184

"I think we need to focus on the open house for the tribe right now," Adam said. "That was a great idea, and I'm really hoping it helps bring some of the less enthusiastic members of the tribe to our side."

Brionna tossed her long brunette hair—nearly the same shade as Charlotte's natural color—over one shoulder. "Honestly, I'm shocked there have been so many upset people. This is a great thing for the community, for their children, and for the tribe's future."

Maybe Little Miss Perfect wasn't so perfect after all. Could she really be so naïve?

"The tribes obviously don't see it that way," Charlotte said. "I've seen this exact same thing happen time and time again. The more traditional members of the community see the invasion of more modern ideals and panic. They worry that it will ruin their way of life. My guess is that's what's happening here. They think if they allow you to educate their children, they'll have to sacrifice generations of tradition in return."

Adam stared at Charlotte, his eyes gazing deeply into hers. "It's exactly that kind of insight we need with this project."

Charlotte cleared her throat, taking a bite of her omelet. "It comes from years of working with these types of situations. When do you have the open house scheduled for?"

"A week from tomorrow," Adam said. "Do you think that's enough time?"

"It's going to have to be," Charlotte said.

For the next hour, they planned the open house while enjoying breakfast. Brionna proved to be organized and intelligent, if a little close-minded at times, and Charlotte grudgingly admitted to herself that she now understood why Adam was working with the hotel heiress.

"Fabulous," Brionna said when they'd finished finalizing the plans. "I know you and Adam will pull things together brilliantly. I can't wait to see the progress you've made when I return from Germany."

"Oh, you're leaving?" Charlotte asked. She hated that her heart gave a happy leap at the news.

"Just for a few days hopefully. There's a problem with one of our properties in Berlin, and I need to go check it out."

Brionna leaned forward, brushing a kiss across Adam's cheek. She laughed at the smudge of lipstick she left there, rubbing it with her finger.

Charlotte stared. What was happening?

Adam had said they weren't together. But Brionna definitely wanted to be.

"Well, have a nice trip," Charlotte said faintly.

"I will." Brionna gave Adam a meaningful look. "Keep me updated."

She strode across the room, and a moment later the door to the suite clicked closed. Charlotte rose as well, grabbing *Pride and Prejudice* from where it rested beside her empty plate and holding it close.

Adam quickly stood, knocking his chair off balance. It teetered on two legs for a moment before crashing back to the ground.

"Charlotte, please," Adam said.

She didn't meet his eyes. "I'd better start on my to-do list so we can be ready for the open house next week. I'll have Becky keep you updated on our progress through either emails or texts."

"That wasn't what it looked like," Adam said, coming around the table. "I don't know why Brionna was so touchy-feely today. It's not like her."

Charlotte took a deep breath, then met Adam's gaze squarely.

"Your relationship with Brionna is of no concern to me. Now if you'll excuse me, I have work to do."

"Let's talk about this," Adam called as Charlotte strode toward the door.

"No time," Charlotte threw over her shoulder.

If only her heart would listen to her brain.

Chapter Eighteen

Charlotte avoided Adam as much as possible over the next week and threw herself into preparing for the open house. She sent communications through Becky instead of texting and emailing Adam herself. The few times they were forced to be in the same room together, Charlotte made sure Becky was there, too, so that Adam wouldn't be tempted to veer into more personal conversations. It wasn't a perfect plan, but so far it had worked.

She kept her phone calls with Emma brief, and each night Charlotte fell into bed completely exhausted and was asleep within moments. But she loved her job, and for the first time in a long time she felt like she had a purpose.

The day of the open house, Charlotte woke up before dawn and sat on the deck to enjoy a cup of warm peppermint tea. She pulled her thin jacket tightly around her body as the breeze cut through her. It still surprised her that a desert could be so cold before the sun rose to warm it once more.

She took a sip of her tea, listening to the sounds of wildlife waking. Birds chirped in the trees, and she could hear the screech of monkeys as well. At first all the animal calls had blended together, but she was getting better at picking out the individual species.

Brionna had been gone all week. In some ways, it had been a relief to not have to worry about playing nice with Little Miss Perfect. But in other ways, Charlotte had wished Brionna was here. It would be so much easier to move on from Adam if he really was with the hotel heiress.

The sun crested the horizon, and Charlotte let out a gasp. Pinks and oranges burst across the sky, illuminating the savanna. She heard the trumpet of an elephant blowing its horn and watched as a lion darted between two trees in the distance.

She held her cup of tea close to her face, savoring these few minutes of peace. Would Adam appreciate a sunrise the way she did, or was he the kind of person who hated mornings? Not that she'd ever find out.

The sliding glass door opened, and Becky stepped onto the porch.

"Good morning, Your Highness," she said. "I've just spoken to Mr. Montgomery. He was wondering if it would be possible to leave for the village an hour early this morning? Just to make sure we have ample time to get everything set up for the open house."

"No problem," Charlotte said. She took a final sip of her peppermint tea, then rose. Her moment of peace was gone, and it was time to get to work.

By the time the last of the colorful posters were loaded into the back of the SUV bound for the village, Charlotte was definitely feeling the pressure. Maybe she'd been too hard on Blessing for cracking under the stress.

For the past week, Charlotte had poured her heart and soul into this school. If, after all her efforts, people still disapproved of the project, she'd be crushed.

"Careful," Charlotte said as one of the hotel employees jammed the edge of a chart outlining how the tribe's traditions would be implemented into the school's curriculum.

"Don't worry so much," came Adam's deep voice from behind. "We've done everything we can to prepare for today. If this doesn't work, it won't be for lack of trying."

Charlotte turned, trying to ignore the way his mere presence could make her entire body shiver. He'd chosen one of his gray suits today, and she loved the way it contrasted with his dark beard and blue eyes. Her mouth felt full of cotton, and she swallowed hard.

"It's difficult not to get caught up in this project."

"It's been your dream for a long time," Adam said. "But that's why I know you're the perfect person to convince everyone we only want to help. Are you ready to go?"

Charlotte nodded, nervously smoothing down her pleated light blue skirt. She'd paired it with a filmy cream-colored blouse and classic heels, wanting to represent the royal family well today. She hoped her position as a princess would be an asset and not a stumbling block.

Adam's warm hand caught her trembling one, giving it a light squeeze. She looked up into his eyes, calmness washing over her.

"You look beautiful," he said, his tone sincere. "And you're going to do great today. Think of how nervous you were before the keynote a couple of weeks ago, and they gave you a standing ovation."

"How did you know I was nervous?"

"Because I know you, Char." He gave her hand one last squeeze, then dropped it. "Let's go."

She got into the car in a daze, forgetting to protest when Adam slid onto the seat beside her. Did Adam really know her that well?

No, that was ridiculous. He'd told her himself that her emotions were always written across her face. He had probably just noticed her nerves when she walked onto the stage for the speech, and the trembling of her hands today. Still, that meant he'd paid attention.

The ten miles to the village flew by. Paved blacktop turned into a compact dirt road. Dust billowed out from the tires, and a rabbit darted across their path.

"It's beautiful, isn't it?" Adam said, motioning to the landscape outside their window.

"I thought you were crazy to move here from Durham," Charlotte admitted. "But I get it now. There's something about this place that I can't quite name, but it's intoxicating."

"I always suspected you'd love it here. I'm glad you came back, Char."

She swallowed hard, knowing she shouldn't admit how much she loved South Africa. Against her will, the words slipped out anyway. "Me too."

The dirt turned to dark brown clay, and Charlotte held onto the door for support as the car bounced over potholes and divots. Grass huts appeared on the horizon. As they drew closer, Charlotte could make out brightly covered rugs hanging from the doorways.

"We're here," Adam said unnecessarily.

Children raced alongside the car, their smiles broad and filled with joy. Their dark skin glistened in the sunlight as they waved enthusiastically.

Charlotte laughed, waving back. The windows were tinted dark enough she was pretty sure they couldn't see, but their excitement was infectious. "At least they don't seem upset we're here. Let's hope everyone else is as happy to see us."

"Hey." Adam grabbed her hand, sending waves of heat up Charlotte's arm. He didn't let go. "Today will be great, because your idea was brilliant. This is just what we need to hopefully put a stop to the vandalism. And once that stops, we can get the school up and running by September first, no problem."

She took a shaky breath. "You make it sound so easy."

"Probably not. But you aren't a quitter, and neither am I." The car door opened, and Adam let go of her hand. "Let's do this."

Her hand felt suddenly cold, and she squeezed her fingers to try to rid herself of the tingles from Adam's touch. Why did her body not understand what her heart knew—that she and Adam were over?

Charlotte accepted Joseph's help out of the car. She was suddenly surrounded by dozens of children. Their dress varied from colorful sarongs tied around their waist, to blue jeans and T-shirts. But their enthusiasm was the same, regardless of fashion. They bounced up and down excitedly, calling, "Princess Charlotte!" in heavily accented English.

For the first time since arriving in South Africa, Charlotte was in her element. She bent down, accepting hugs from the children. Each tiny pair of arms that wrapped around her waist or neck erased some of her tension.

She knew how to do this—how to connect with the children. It reminded her why she was here, working so hard to make sure this school opened.

Someone pushed aside the door flap of the nearest hut, and Chief Mandla emerged. Gone was the black suit and white shirt she'd seen him in at the conference, replaced by more traditional clothing. A cheetah pelt hung over his shoulders like a necklace, making a *v* so that his sides were exposed. His skirt looked as though it had been sewn from lion fur, and he wore a headband with white feathers pluming out of it.

"Princess Charlotte." He dropped into a low bow, then rose. "Welcome to my village. It is our pleasure to welcome you here."

Charlotte extended her hand, and Chief Mandla shook it warmly. She was no longer Charlotte, but instead the princess of Durham.

"It is an honor, Chief Mandla," she said. "I bring you the warmest regards from my parents, His Royal Majesty King Geoffrey and Her Majesty Queen Nicolette."

"I accept them gladly," Chief Mandla said.

Adam stepped forward, and the two men exchanged a warm handshake. That surprised Charlotte.

Adam had told her the chief had been a big help since the school began construction, but she'd assumed things would be tense between them. The School Montgomery was behind schedule, and someone in the tribe was vandalizing the property. But the two men greeted each other like friends.

"I do hope today helps the situation," the chief said, his voice low. "Thank you both for being willing to try."

Adam clapped the older man on the shoulder. "With Her Highness on our side, we can't possibly fail. Where would you like us to do the presentation?"

As Charlotte directed the hotel staff where to set up the various easels and poster boards, she felt herself relax even further. The children danced around her, chattering in a language she didn't understand. Parents would occasionally scold someone for getting in the way with a sharp command, but Charlotte always offered a kind smile in return and said she didn't mind. And she truly didn't. The children were a constant reminder of why this school had to open.

It was a blessedly cool summer day. The sky was overcast, and a breeze kept upsetting the posters but made the temperature rather pleasant. As the villagers gathered, Charlotte saw a variety of expressions on their faces—everything from open excitement to cautious interest to outright hostility. But that was okay. People might still be upset after their presentation, but at least they'd have all the facts.

The village was organized with huts on the outer circle and a large common area in the center. Chief Mandla had instructed them to set up the presentation there. As the time for the presentation to begin grew closer, people started gathering on the soft dirt. Adults sat together, talking in low voices, while the children ran across the space, settling down next to an adult only to pop back up a few moments later to move to sit by someone else.

Chief Mandla stepped between Adam and Charlotte, looking back and forth between them. "Are you ready for this?"

Adam looked at Charlotte, his gaze electric. She gave a slight nod.

"Yes," Adam confirmed. "Let's do this."

Chief Mandla stepped forward and raised his hands. The crowd quieted down, and he started speaking in his native tongue.

"He's thanking everyone for coming today," the translator said in a low voice. "Explaining how important the school is and introducing the two of you." The translator paused, listening. Chief Mandla stepped back, extending a hand toward them, and the translator said, "He's turning the time over to you."

"You've got this," Adam mouthed to Charlotte. She took a deep breath and stepped forward.

"Thank you for joining us here today," Charlotte said. She paused, giving the translator time to relay her words before continuing. "My colleague and I are very excited to share our plans for the School Montgomery, and we'll stick around as long as necessary to answer any of your questions."

For the next two hours, Adam and Charlotte explained their vision for the school and relayed their plans. Charlotte loved watching the faces of the crowd turn from open distrust to cautious excitement as she spoke, and by the end, she had a feeling that the school would encounter much less resistance from here on out. At least, she hoped it would. They'd done their absolute best to calm everyone's fears. That was all they could do.

The staff began packing up the posters and easels as the tribe members went back to whatever they'd been doing before the presentation began. Chief Mandla walked over to Charlotte and Adam.

"I cannot thank you enough for this open house," he said. "I think it really helped. Hopefully, there will be no more issues with vandalism at the school."

"It was our pleasure," Charlotte said.

"We'll be in touch." Adam clapped the chief on the back, then he and Charlotte got into the car and left the village behind.

Adam pulled Charlotte to him in a fierce hug, dropping a kiss on her head. "You were amazing back there, Char."

Her cheeks were warm, and she self-consciously brushed her hair back behind her ears. "You weren't so bad yourself. I think that it went really, really well."

"I'm not sure everyone's completely on board, but I think even those who don't want to send their children to the school at least understand now that we aren't a threat."

"We'll do another open house when the school is completed," Charlotte said. "A big celebration especially for the tribe. They can come and see the finished product and meet the teachers. Now that the open house is behind us, we really need to go through the applications and start setting up interviews . . ."

"Shh." Adam put a finger to her lips, then quickly pulled it away, as though just realizing what he'd done. "This is the first positive news we've had on the project in nearly a year. Let's just enjoy it."

"I am enjoying it," Charlotte said. "But September first isn't that far away, and the school's construction is still extremely behind schedule."

"Are you going to paint the walls yourself?" Adam asked.

Charlotte folded her arms, unable to stop herself from smiling. "If I have to."

"We need to celebrate this, Char. And don't tell me there's no time for it, because I know for a fact that you cleared your schedule for the entire day in case the open house took longer than planned."

"I don't know. I'm sure I could find something to do back at the hotel."

"Come celebrate with me instead." Adam leaned forward, his blue eyes pulling her in. "Take a break. You've earned it."

She should tell him no and go back to the hotel. It was the smart thing to do.

"I guess a successful open house is cause for celebration."

Why had she said that?

Adam nodded eagerly. "Let me take you to the elephant reserve. I know you'll love it, and you really can't come to South Africa without spending time there."

She did want to see the elephants, and who knew when she'd have another opportunity? Charlotte took a deep breath and prayed she wouldn't regret this. "That does sound nice. Let's go."

Chapter Nineteen

$\mathcal{A}$dam barely dared glance at Charlotte during the drive to the elephant sanctuary. She was like a skittish colt, and he worried that any miscalculation on his part would have her demanding the driver turn right back around and take her to the hotel.

She'd been avoiding him. That much had become obvious since her return to South Africa. But after the success they'd had with the open house, Adam had decided to push his luck and invite her to the elephant reserve. He still couldn't believe she'd agreed.

"How many elephants are on the reserve?" Charlotte asked.

It was the first thing she'd said since agreeing to come with him, and Adam hurried to respond.

"About twelve," he said. "It's still relatively small. The reserve only opened five years ago, and they only house elephants who are too sick or injured to return to the wild. A few years back they welcomed a male to the herd, and last summer the first baby elephant was born at the sanctuary."

"Amazing," Charlotte said, her tone almost reverent. "I read about it online, of course, but I can't wait to see the sanctuary in person."

The trees overhead grew dense, blocking out the sunlight and casting shadows across Charlotte's face. Adam loved the easy conversation flowing between them now. He ached to lean forward, cradle her face in his hands, and brush his lips across hers. But he wouldn't push her. Right now, he just hoped that today would be an important first step to healing their relationship.

An iron archway parted the trees, announcing the entrance to the sanctuary. The car pulled to a halt in the gravel parking lot, and a moment later Joseph opened the door.

Charlotte stepped out of the car, and Adam was right behind her. She stood still with her hands tightly clasped as she stared up at the trees. The air around them was hushed. Birds chirped in the treetops, and the dry savanna seemed more humid and jungle-like here. An almost invisible layer of steam clung to the green branches of the trees and bushes surrounding them. Adam was suddenly glad he'd left his suit jacket and tie in the car.

When Charlotte spoke, her voice was reverent. "I didn't realize it would be this beautiful."

"The photos don't quite do it justice," Adam agreed.

She took a deep breath, turning her face toward the sky. "I feel like we've entered another world."

Adam wished he were brave enough to ask if it was a world where they could be together. The late afternoon heat wrapped around them like a cocoon, making him feel like anything was possible. Even a future with the princess of Durham.

Adam swallowed hard, then held out a hand to Charlotte. They said actions spoke louder than words, right? He was going to test that theory today.

Charlotte's blue eyes met his, wide and unreadable. Adam held his breath, praying he hadn't just ruined everything. She might stomp back to the car and leave him in a cloud of dust. He wouldn't even blame her for it.

She didn't leave. Instead, Charlotte carefully placed her hand in his. It was soft and cool, despite the heat of the day.

Adam closed his hand around hers, heart hammering furiously as hope blossomed in his chest. Her action was so small, but he felt the significance of it like a weight.

He didn't say anything as he led her down the tree-lined path. If he talked about what had just happened, she might remember that they no longer did things like hold hands. The pathway was empty, no doubt thanks to Joseph and Karla, and grew more shaded the further they walked.

"Do you come here often?" Charlotte asked. Her voice was low and quiet, making the hairs on the back of Adam's neck prickle.

"Not as often as I'd like to," Adam said. "I think this is my third or fourth visit to the sanctuary. It's peaceful here, and I always feel more ready to face the world after a few hours with the elephants."

Charlotte glanced up at Adam, then back at the pathway. Her eyelashes fluttered against her cheeks, creating little half-moons. "It's very picturesque. I imagine everyone who stays at your hotel wants to visit the sanctuary."

The words were right, but the tone was all wrong—tight and a little unsure. He'd learned to read her moods during their hours spent together in Durham and had only refined that skill as they worked together on the school. "Is something bothering you?"

Charlotte looked up at him quickly, then away again. "No, I'm fine. Just thinking."

He nudged her shoulder lightly with his own, tightening his grip on her hand. "That's a dangerous pastime for someone as smart as you."

She rolled her eyes, but a smile curved the corners of her mouth. "Do you flatter all the girls you take here like this, or just me?"

So that's what she was worrying about. Adam stopped in the middle of the pathway, and Charlotte reluctantly turned to face him. But she wouldn't meet his eyes and instead stared fixedly at the tree roots criss-crossing the dirt path.

"Look at me, Char," Adam said quietly.

She slowly lifted her eyes to meet his. The blues of her irises were darker than normal, her expression guarded. "What?"

"I've never taken any woman here but you. Well, and my mother. But I don't think that counts." His mom had been very sick by that point, and they'd all known death was on the horizon. But a few weeks before the end, she'd woken up feeling energized and asked to see the sanctuary.

It was one of his last happy memories of his mother. He hadn't wanted to share that with anyone—until Charlotte.

"Brionna's never been?" Charlotte asked.

Adam brought her hand to his lips, brushing a soft kiss across the knuckles. "Not with me. If she's visited the sanctuary, it's been on her own. This place is too special for me to share with just anyone."

Charlotte tucked a strand of hair behind one ear, nodding. Her hair had grown a bit since she'd first come to South Africa, exposing the dark roots underneath. No doubt the palace wouldn't approve of the look, but Adam thought she was beautiful no matter what.

"Okay," Charlotte said, nodding. "You didn't have to tell me that, but thank you."

He wanted to tell her that she meant the world to him. That he'd never felt so deeply for another person. That he loved her.

But he also didn't want to freak her out, so he tugged her forward without saying a word. Maybe it was his imagination, but he thought her grip was a little more relaxed, and her steps a little lighter.

Adam's heart felt lighter, too. For the first time in a long time, he felt hope.

The path rounded a corner. Adam quickened his steps, suddenly eager to share this with Charlotte. The trees thinned, and the sound of rushing water grew louder.

Adam pulled Charlotte through the trees and into the clearing. She gasped, her hand tightening on his and eyes growing wide. A watering hole stood before them, sunlight sparkling off its clear blue surface. Water cascaded down a rock formation, creating a fifteen-foot high waterfall. Beneath the water stood a small elephant, its size clearly indicating it was still a baby. Its trunk was raised into the air, spraying water toward the woman in a uniform standing before her.

"This is incredible," Charlotte breathed. "Idyllic."

"Yeah," Adam agreed. He smiled at Charlotte. "Want to help give the elephant a bath?"

"They'll let us do that?"

Adam would give the sanctuary anything they wanted if it made Charlotte's eyes light up like this. He couldn't resist bringing her hand to his lips and placing a soft kiss in the center of her palm. "I guess this is another one of those side effects of being a princess— you get to play with baby elephants."

She laughed, pulling him toward the handler. "I'd call it more of a perk. Come on, let's go meet her."

"How do you know the elephant's not a him?" Adam teased.

"Women know these things intuitively."

The handler waved at them, a wide-brimmed hat hiding most of her face. She was a slight woman, with darkly tanned skin and sun-kissed hair that hung halfway down her back in a ponytail. The bottoms of her khaki shorts were damp from the pond.

"Welcome," she called, her words heavily accented. "Please, come join me. Evening Star can't wait to meet you."

Charlotte bit her lip, quickly covering the last few yards to the handler. Adam laughed, following closely behind her.

"She's beautiful," Charlotte said. "How old is she?"

"Nearly a year old now," the handler said. "It is such an honor to meet you, Princess Charlotte. I am Nali."

Adam gave Charlotte a sly look. "Is Evening Star a boy?"

"No, a female," Nali said.

Charlotte raised one eyebrow at Adam, her expression clearly saying *I told you so.* But her lips were soft, her expression teasing. "She's beautiful. It's so nice to meet you, Nali. How long have you worked at the sanctuary?"

"Since the day it opened," Nali said. She stepped deeper into the pond, moving away from the shore where Adam and Charlotte stood. Evening Star sprayed Nali with another blast of water, and the handler laughed. "She's a very playful baby and loves visitors. Would you like to come into the water and help me bathe her?"

"Oh, I don't know." Charlotte flicked a glance behind her, to where Joseph and Karla stood. They looked uncomfortably hot in their black suits and ties, their expressions dour.

"Come on, Char," Adam said. He lowered his voice so that only she could hear. "We're all alone. You don't have to be a princess here."

She glanced at the elephant, then back to Adam. "I don't know," she said, her voice unsure.

"Don't worry about getting close to the animals," Nali said encouragingly. "Evening Star especially is very gentle, and I'll stay right beside you to make sure nothing happens."

But Adam knew that wasn't what Charlotte was worried about. She'd spent a lifetime being prim and proper. Letting go didn't come easily for her.

Evening Star lifted her trunk again, letting out a trumpet. She rose on her hind legs, ears lifted, and splashed playfully back down, soaking Nali. Charlotte clapped her hands to her mouth, shoulders shaking with laughter.

A jet of water flew through the air, hitting Charlotte right in the face. She gasped and sputtered, her hair hanging limply around her face and blouse pressed against her body.

"Char!" Adam said, going to her side.

Joseph and Karla took a step forward, but Charlotte held up a hand. "I'm fine."

Nali leaned over, bracing her hands on her knees as tears of mirth streamed down her face. "I am so sorry, Princess," she gasped. "I should have warned you. Evening Star can be a rascal when she wants to be."

Charlotte pulled her blouse away from her body, grinning up at Adam. "It's okay. I can't believe I just got sprayed in the face by an African elephant."

"Elephant spit looks good on you." He couldn't resist brushing a strand of wet hair behind one of her ears, letting his fingers linger against her cheekbone.

Charlotte bit her lip, but she didn't move away. "Check your facts—it's clearly water, not elephant spit."

"Water that's been in an elephant's nose. So perhaps you're right—it's more accurate to call it snot than spit."

"Princesses don't deal with snot or spit," Charlotte said with faux indignation.

Adam ran a hand over her shoulder and down her arm until their hands were linked. "Whatever you say, Your Highness."

Nali laughed again, shaking her head. "I get doused about once a shift. But the African sun is so hot that you'll dry off in no time. I think Evening Star likes you. Want to come pet her?"

Charlotte took a cautious step forward. Water squished from her heels into the soft mud at the edge of the pond.

"Take off your shoes and get into the water with her," Nali encouraged. "It's only about a meter high at the deepest point."

"Oh, I don't know," Charlotte said, fisting a hand against her heart. "Maybe I'd better watch from here."

Determinedly, Adam slipped out of his shoe and carefully peeled away his sock. He let his foot squish into the soft mud, balancing precariously as he slipped off his other shoe and sock.

"What are you doing?" Charlotte asked in alarm.

"I'm going to play with Evening Star." Adam rolled up the cuffs of his pants until they were nearly to his knees, then did the same with his shirt sleeves. "Come with me."

"Adam." She lowered her voice, eyes glancing around furtively.

"Joseph and Karla won't let anyone near enough to take a photo. We're the only ones here, Char." He held out a hand, stretched toward hers in a silent invitation. "Trust me."

He held his breath as Evening Star splashed in the pond behind him. Would she accept his invitation, or turn and run away?

Slowly, Charlotte stepped out of first one heel, then the other. Her feet and calves were bare, and the soft mud squished between her toes. A furrow between her brow told him she was anxious, but Charlotte walked the few feet between them and placed her soft hand in his.

"Okay. Let's go play with Evening Star."

Chapter Twenty

Charlotte wiggled her toes in the mud, relishing the feel of the warm earth caking her feet. Adam's hand was sure and firm, his eyes never leaving hers as he tugged her forward.

She was insane for doing this. Adam had broken her heart, and while he said he wasn't interested in dating Brionna, that still didn't change the past.

Her foot touched the water, and she let out a gasp. It was colder than she'd anticipated, instantly bringing down her internal temperature.

"It's colder than I thought it would be," Charlotte said, still watching Adam.

"You'll get used to it soon," Nali called. Charlotte had almost forgotten the handler was there.

"I'll keep you warm," Adam said quietly, pulling her closer to his side.

Charlotte let him. Her eyes traced the planes of his face, the warmth of his smile, the strong cut of his jaw.

Adam pulled her deeper into the pond. The water lapped against the hem of her skirt, nearly to her knees now. But Charlotte was committed, and what's more, she didn't want to turn back.

Evening Star was within touching distance now. She raised her trunk in the air, letting out another burst of water. Charlotte laughed, ducking down to avoid the worst of the blast. Her sleeve brushed the water, but what did it matter? She was already soaked. Adam crouched down with her, grinning, but the spray of water grazed one of his shoulders.

"Evening Star," Adam said in a tone of mock severity. "What was that? I thought we were friends."

Charlotte laughed, resting a hand tentatively on the animal's belly. The skin was slick with water, and a little rough. Evening Star snorted, her ears flapping forward.

Adam came up behind Charlotte and placed his hand next to hers. "Hey, girl," he said in a quiet voice.

His breath caressed Charlotte's ear, making her shiver. Evening Star took a step back, and Adam's chest brushed against Charlotte's back as the animal jostled them.

"This is incredible," Adam whispered.

Charlotte could only nod. "Did your mother get to do this?"

"No, she didn't get in the water. We were worried she'd catch a cold, even with the warm temperatures."

The elephant shifted again, making the water lap around their legs. Charlotte turned to face Adam, their faces mere inches apart.

"You miss her," she said. It wasn't a question.

"Every day," Adam agreed. "She was my hero."

The air between them crackled with tension. Adam leaned forward, his eyes intense.

He was going to kiss her. Charlotte held her breath, not sure if she wanted him to. What about Brionna? What about the way he'd broken her heart?

But people changed. Adam had changed, and so had she.

She couldn't take the tension any longer. Charlotte bent down, scooping up a handful of water and flicking it in Adam's face.

His eyes widened as he brushed the drops out of his eyes. Charlotte put a hand to her mouth, shoulders shaking with laughter.

"I can't believe a princess would do something like that," Adam said.

"You said I wasn't a princess here." Charlotte scooped up another handful of water and threw it.

Adam let out a growl, lunging forward. Charlotte shrieked and danced away, while Evening Star blasted another jet of water into the air.

"Oh no you don't." Adam's arm snaked around Charlotte's waist, pulling her flush against his body. She rested her hands on his arms, intending to squirm away.

Droplets of water clung to the dark hairs of his beard, beading on his upper lip. Charlotte tightened her hold on him, feeling the firm muscles of his biceps beneath her hands. Water lapped at her legs, tugging at the hem of her skirt and making it cling to her knees.

She wanted to stay in this moment forever.

Charlotte cleared her throat, looking away. Adam dropped his hold, and Charlotte made her way to Evening Star's other side, where Nali stood.

"Did you say you were going to give her a bath?" Charlotte asked. "We'd love to help."

For the next hour they played with Evening Star. Charlotte and Adam scrubbed down the elephant's thick skin, becoming completely soaked in the process. Then Nali coaxed the baby out of the pool and taught Charlotte and Adam how to examine the pads of her feet and check her nails for any issues. Charlotte gave herself over to the experience, wanting to just enjoy the moment for once in her life.

Nali had been right—their clothes quickly dried in the hot African sun as they helped the keeper take measurements of Evening Star for the sanctuary's veterinarian. There was a rustle in the trees behind them, and Charlotte looked over her shoulder to see another elephant emerge from the jungle.

216

This elephant was much larger than Evening Star. Whereas the baby was about the same height as Charlotte, this newcomer towered above her. Charlotte stared in awe as the elephant lumbered past her and wrapped a trunk around the baby elephant's waist, almost as though the two were hugging.

"This is Morning Star," Nali said, running a hand down the animal's trunk. "She's Evening Star's mother."

"Ah." Charlotte smiled. "Clever names. I like them."

Nali patted Morning Star's side. "This one has a much calmer temperament than her baby. See how she stands so still?"

Adam reached forward, his arm brushing Charlotte's as he patted the mama elephant's belly. As tall as he was, he barely reached the animal's shoulder. "She's beautiful."

"Would you like to ride her?" Nali asked.

Ride an elephant? Charlotte glanced at Adam, her excitement mirrored in his grin.

"We're allowed to do that?" Charlotte asked.

"Sure," Nali said. She glanced over at Joseph and Karla. "It's perfectly safe. We let tourists do it all the time."

Adam raised his eyebrows in question. "Want to?"

Charlotte nodded eagerly. "Absolutely. Emma is going to be so jealous."

Had Charlotte ever had such a perfect day?

Nali said something to Morning Star, and the elephant bent down on her front knees. "Climb on up," Nali said cheerfully.

Charlotte eyed the elephant. "How do we stay on?"

"Oh, she'll move slowly enough for you to balance easily. It isn't hard."

"I won't let you fall," Adam said. "Can I help you up?"

Charlotte glanced over at Joseph and Karla, but they both seemed at ease—well, as at ease as they ever looked. Charlotte wasn't about to pass up this opportunity. "Yes, thank you."

Adam nodded, placing his hands on the curve of her waist. His touch sent tendrils of heat creeping up her spine, and she took a shaky breath. Adam boosted her onto the animal, and Charlotte straddled her, careful to keep her skirt tucked around her legs. Morning Star shifted, and Charlotte felt the animal's powerful muscles beneath her own legs with the movement.

In a moment, Adam was behind her. The sharp scent of the animal made Charlotte's nose sting, while the hard planes of Adam's body pressed against her back made her palms sweaty and mouth suddenly dry.

"Hold on," Nali said. She spoke to the elephant, and it rose back onto its feet.

Charlotte squealed. Adam's arm wrapped around her waist and she clutched at his hand with one of hers, using the other to help balance on the animal. Morning Star lumbered forward, her movements slow yet exhilarating.

"I can't believe it," Charlotte breathed. "I'm riding an elephant in Africa. I can't believe it."

Adam's arm tightened around her, and his lips pressed into her hair. "I can't believe I get to experience this with you."

She couldn't stop herself from leaning back into him. Her fingers played with the black hairs on his arm as Morning Star walked around the pond. Nali walked beside them, giving the animal commands as they headed down a path. Evening Star trotted behind them, following her mother closely.

Charlotte threw out her arms, letting her head fall back and eyes drift closed.

Morning Star stumbled over a rock, shifting beneath them. Charlotte squealed, bringing her arms back in and clutching at Adam's hold on her.

"It's okay," Adam whispered in her ear. "I've got you, Char. I've got you."

Her body relaxed against his, though she hadn't given it permission to do so. Adam made her feel safe and secure, and she knew he wouldn't let anything bad happen to her.

"Okay," she whispered. "I trust you."

She heard his breathing hitch, then grow slow and even once more. But his hold tightened on her even more, and she knew he'd felt the significance of her words.

Charlotte didn't know when things had changed. But she did trust Adam. No, she more than trusted him.

She loved him.

The realization crashed into her, stealing her breath. She. Loved. Him. And she trusted Adam— maybe not completely, but enough to hope that a relationship between them might be possible.

Charlotte was so caught up in her thoughts that she was barely aware of Nali instructing Morning Star to halt. The animal kneeled down again, and Adam climbed off.

He held his arms out to Charlotte in silent invitation. She slid into them without hesitation, feeling his strong hands circle her waist.

Her feet touched the ground, but Adam's hands didn't leave her waist. Charlotte rested hers gently against his chest, feeling the frantic beating of his heart.

"Char," Adam said, his voice husky.

She slid her hands up his chest and behind his neck, locking them there.

Adam's eyes searched hers, as though asking for permission. Charlotte took a step closer, aching for the feel of his lips on hers.

That was all the invitation Adam needed. His head lowered toward hers, and she let her eyes flutter closed.

Adam's mouth covered hers, his lips soft and warm and sweet. She pressed closer, threading her fingers into his hair. Adam's mouth suddenly became insistent, weaving a spell of magic over her that she never wanted broken.

Kissing Adam had always been as easy as breathing. How had they ever let this go?

Adam leaned his forehead against hers, his breath ragged and eyes filled with a million different emotions.

"I don't know how I ever let you go," he whispered.

"You were an idiot."

He chuckled, dropping a soft kiss on her lips. "You'll get no argument from me."

She let her hands slide down to his chest, feeling the frenetic beating of his heart beneath her palm. "I didn't think that was going to happen today."

"Me either. But I'm not complaining." His eyes darkened, and he cupped her cheek with his hand. "I love you, Charlotte. And this time, I'm not letting you go."

She sucked in a breath, her pulse making her ears rush with blood. His hand was gentle against her cheek, the pads of his fingers a little rough, just like she remembered.

Love. Could he really return her feelings?

"Don't say that," she whispered.

221

Behind them the elephants snorted, following the sound of Nali's voice as she led mother and baby away. But Adam didn't flinch. Didn't move his gaze from Charlotte's even for a moment.

"Would you rather that I lie?" he asked. "I think I loved you even back in Durham. But I was scared."

She didn't know how, but somehow her hand was clutching his, keeping his warm palm pressed to her cheek. "What were you afraid of?"

"You. How deeply I felt for you, and so quickly. And I won't deny that your family obligations are intimidating."

The summer heat was suddenly suffocating, and Charlotte's entire body felt hot. She dropped his hand, taking a step away from Adam. Cool air rushed in to meet the space where his hand had been moments before, soothing some of the heat from her cheeks.

"I can't change who I am. I will always be a princess."

He put an arm around her waist, reeling her back toward him. "I know. And I don't care anymore. I want you, Char. Every part of you. Every side—the princess included. Becoming a part of your world wouldn't be a sacrifice. It would be an honor."

The words were right. Charlotte saw the sincerity in Adam's eyes. But she could feel herself pulling inward, trying to build the walls back around her heart that he'd sent crashing down.

She brushed away a tear, hating how her voice shook. "You broke my heart when you left."

"I know." He buried his face in her neck, tightening his hold on her. "Let me make it up to you. I was a stupid, cowardly git."

She half laughed, half sobbed. Charlotte couldn't deny him anymore. She put a hand on his cheek, feeling the soft scruff of his beard against her palm, and raised his face to meet hers. The regret in his eyes tore at her soul, but filled it somehow, too.

He loved her. Loved. Her.

Charlotte rose on her tiptoes, pressing her lips to his. She had intended for the kiss to be chaste, but emotion flared inside her at his hungry response. His hands were at her waist, in her hair, cradling her face, running along her arms. She drank him in, pulling him impossibly closer.

Eventually she had to pull away. Charlotte rested her hands on Adam's arms, steadying herself as she gulped in oxygen. Her entire body tingled with awareness, and she wanted nothing more than to drag his lips to hers once more.

But Adam didn't go in for another kiss. Instead, he tenderly tucked a strand of hair behind her ear, the love in his eyes wrapping around her like a blanket.

"I love you," he repeated, his voice soft and quiet. "And I'm going to tell you that every day."

Charlotte took a deep breath. It was time to trust Adam again. To take a risk. To give him her heart. This time, he seemed ready to accept it.

"I love you, too."

Chapter Twenty-One

The next week passed as though it were a dream, and Adam felt like the luckiest man alive. He spent his days working on the school with Charlotte, and in the evenings they'd sit out on his veranda, listening to the chirp of crickets and watching the stars sparkle overhead in between stolen kisses.

It was like the best form of déjà vu. He felt like he'd been transported back in time to those ten magical days in Durham, and it was absolutely wonderful.

He still couldn't believe that Charlotte loved him.

The only dark spot in his newly rekindled relationship with Charlotte was Brionna. She was still looking at properties all over South Africa, which Adam counted as a blessing since she was often gone. He did his best to reassure Charlotte that his relationship with

Brionna was purely platonic, but she still grew tense every time the subject was brought up—usually by a hotel employee who wanted Brionna's input on something. When Brionna returned, Adam would tell her about his relationship with Charlotte. But for now, he was enjoying the secret love bubble the two of them had created.

Adam walked briskly toward his office, feeling the weight of the school project more than he had all week. In just a few hours, they'd hold another tour of the school. This time, the entire tribal council would be in attendance—and hopefully they'd leave with smiles on their face instead of stomping out in a cloud of anger.

The construction crew had worked tirelessly all week, trying to get as far as possible on the project before the tour. Adam had been awake before the sun and gone to sleep long after it set every day, and he knew that Charlotte had been on the same sleep-deprived schedule. But it would all be worth it if they could win over the council once and for all with today's tour. After the success of the open house, Adam was hopeful.

He strode into his office, sinking into his office chair and waking up his computer. It was a little after nine in the morning, and he was anxious to read the night guards' daily report. Twice in the past week they'd heard suspicious noises, but both times a search of the building had turned up nothing. Since no further vandalism had occurred, Adam was hopeful that it was just a combination of overly anxious guards and typical nighttime noises.

He scanned the report, shoulders relaxing as he read the three short sentences that soothed his nerves. Last night had been uneventful, which was just what Adam wanted to hear.

This school meant so much to Charlotte. There were so many reasons the project couldn't fail, but breaking Charlotte's heart again was at the top of the list.

A knock sounded at the door, then it swung open. Keith walked into the office, a thick manila envelope in his hands.

"This just came for you," Keith said, setting it on the desk. "Certified mail. The front desk signed for it, but I told them I'd bring it to you since I was headed here anyway."

Adam frowned, sliding the package closer. It was nearly two inches thick and felt like the interior was padded with bubble wrap. "Who's it from?"

Keith shrugged, dropping into a chair. "You weren't expecting it?"

"No." Adam read the return address, his hands growing clammy at the familiar location.

This was from the family home in Durham. The one where Adam had grown up. Where his mother had

227

spent most of her time until she and his father moved to South Africa.

Adam swallowed, his mind racing. What could possibly be in this envelope? His father hadn't mentioned any package—not that they'd talked more than a few minutes at a time since Adam asked to go to the wedding—and besides, he was pretty sure his father hadn't been back to their ancestral home since the funeral.

Whatever it was, Adam didn't want to open the package in front of Keith. He rested his hands casually over the return address, looking at Keith expectantly. "Did you need something?"

"Just to confirm that you want to start the tour at two o'clock this afternoon," Keith said. "The general contractor wants to make sure they've got everything as tidy as possible by then. They're hoping to finish up another coat of paint on the second floor."

"That should be fine," Adam said. "Tell them that the council knows it's an active construction site. We can give the tour around the crew while they work. I don't want to lose momentum now."

Keith nodded, rising from his chair. "Will do, boss. Need anything else from me before I head over to the school to relay the message?"

"No, I think that's it." Adam's eyes flickered again to the envelope. It looked like someone had shoved an entire novel in the package. What was it? "Thanks again, Keith."

"No problem," Keith said.

Adam waited until the door clicked shut before flipping the envelope over and sliding his index finger underneath the flap. The adhesive was sticky and difficult, but Adam didn't want to risk using scissors and cutting whatever lay inside.

The last of the flap finally pulled free, and a thick stack of papers slid out—five manila envelopes, these ones with tabs. Paper clipped to the first one was a handwritten note on the home's official stationery.

Adam didn't recognize the handwriting, but that didn't stop his heart from pounding furiously in his chest as he read the note.

Dear Mr. Montgomery,

Last week, at the request of Lord Nottingshire, I had the honor of going through Lady Nottingshire's office. While going through the contents of her file cabinet, I found these folders with your name on them. After speaking to His Lordship, he instructed me to forward the files on to you. I have done so with pleasure and hope that this package finds you well.

Please accept my condolences on the loss of your mother. She was a wonderful woman, and we've felt her loss greatly at Nottingshire.

Cordially yours,
Mrs. Wells

Mrs. Wells . . . The name rang a faint bell in Adam's memory. Wasn't she the head housekeeper at Nottingshire Hall? He hadn't spent much time there since he'd moved to Castlebridge for preparatory school. The ancestral home was in the Durham countryside, far from any of the Montgomery Hotels & Resorts properties. Adam hadn't found many reasons to venture back there. The last time had been, what, five years ago? Six, perhaps?

He set the note aside with shaking hands, revealing his mother's familiar cursive. She'd written in black marker on the outside of the folder.

Adam's mouth went dry at the words. *Montgomery-Cartwright Hotel: Adam and Brionna's suite.*

He flipped open the folder, his entire body suddenly clammy with sweat.

A blueprint stared up at him. It was a three-bedroom suite, similar to those in other Montgomery hotels, with one notable exception.

One of the bedrooms had been labeled *nursery*.

Adam thumbed through the papers, his heart beating rapidly. There were color swatches for fabric, paint chips in various hues of gray, and printouts of design possibilities.

He set aside the folder and picked up the one underneath it. The first page was a printout of four possible logos. Each one said Montgomery-Cartwright on it.

Adam didn't have time to go through the stack of folders, nearly two inches thick. But he pored over them anyway as tears pressed at his eyes.

He'd always known that his mother liked Brionna. She'd tried to get the two of them together for years. But he'd had no idea she was so certain that one day he and Brionna would be a couple.

Mother's research had been thorough. She'd included potential property locations all over Europe, noting in the margins the ones already owned by Montgomery or Cartwright, but not yet developed. Schematics for a twenty-story high-rise took up one entire folder. There were pages of notes on cost analysis.

Adam had never suspected that his mother had actually planned his future with Brionna. Mother had obviously spent months on this project, and her loving attention to detail was evident on every page. How long ago had she done this?

He squeezed his eyes tightly shut and pinched the bridge of his nose, willing the tears not to fall. A glance at the clock told him the tour of the school would start in less than two hours now.

These past few days with Charlotte had been practically perfect—so wonderful, in fact, that he'd almost forgotten how much his mother had wanted him and Brionna to get together. But now the evidence of her desires was staring him right in the face.

He closed the last folder and firmly stacked them back on top of each other. It didn't matter what his mother had wanted. Adam loved Charlotte, not Brionna—end of discussion. Still, this life his mother had envisioned for him—one in which she was still very much alive—hurt Adam's heart. Had his father known about this? Doubtful.

Adam dropped the stack of folders into one of his desk drawers and shut it firmly, locking away the memories.

In his car, he rolled down the windows, letting the hot breeze help clear his head as he made the short drive to the school.

The construction crew had done a fantastic job— amazing the progress they could make without vandals constantly setting them back with their destruction. Adam glanced around the front entrance, then wandered through the first floor. All of the walls were taped and mudded, and it looked like the crew had managed to get a second coat of paint applied everywhere.

The click of heels against plywood broke through the hiss of an air compressor and *clip-clip-clip* of a nail gun somewhere on the second floor. Adam turned, his spirits lifting at the sight of Charlotte.

She wore her hard hat without complaint now, but still looked every bit the princess in her flowing navy blue sundress. He quickly crossed the room and greeted her with a long kiss. Adam relished the feel of her lips surrendering to his, and the way she pressed into him had his pulse pounding.

Charlotte set her hands on his chest, pulling away. Her cheeks glowed a soft pink, and she bit her lip and looked down.

"We shouldn't do that here," she said.

"I don't care who sees us together." Adam pulled her in for another kiss.

Unbidden, the blueprint of the suite his mother had designed for him and Brionna flashed into Adam's mind, making him nauseous.

Charlotte took a step back and Adam let her, feeling uneasy.

She clasped her hands together, looking around the room. "The crew's making good time now."

"Yeah, the school looks great," Adam agreed.

His mother had loved Brionna, true. But she'd never met Charlotte. If Mother could only see how great he and Charlotte were together.

"I'm so nervous," Charlotte said. "The last school tour didn't exactly go well."

"That's because I didn't have you on my side," Adam said. "I really think the open house addressed a lot of the worries everyone had. Today's just an opportunity to show them we're on track to open the school on September first."

"You're right." Charlotte straightened Adam's tie, then dropped her hands to her side. "How are you always so calm?"

Adam opened his mouth to respond, but a familiar voice echoed across the room.

"Hello? Adam, are you here?"

Charlotte's eyes widened as the muffled sounds of the front door being shut reached them.

"Is that who I think it is?" Charlotte asked in a low voice.

Adam's stomach writhed as though he'd swallowed a nest of snakes. "She said she wouldn't be back until the weekend."

"There you are." Brionna sauntered across the room, looking professional as always in a crisp black skirt and spring green blouse. Had she lightened her hair? It didn't seem as dark as before.

Adam gasped as Brionna pulled him to her in a tight hug, pinning his arms to his sides. He glanced helplessly over her shoulder at Charlotte. Her arms were folded now, lips pursed into a tight frown.

"It's so good to be back," Brionna said. She rose on her tiptoes, pressing a firm kiss to his cheek.

What was happening? Adam felt frozen, unable to move, as Brionna laughed. She licked her thumb, rubbing at the spot where she'd kissed him.

"Oops. I didn't mean to get lipstick on you. Sorry about that."

Charlotte's eyes narrowed even further and Adam quickly took a step away from Brionna. What was she doing?

Adam cleared his throat. "I wasn't expecting you back so soon."

"I cut my trip short because I chose a property." Brionna's eyes brightened, and she clutched at his arm. "It's absolutely perfect, Adam. You have to come out there with me sometime. As soon as I saw it, I knew there was no point in looking at anything else. We sign the papers next week."

"That's great," Adam said weakly.

Brionna nodded, looking back and forth between him and Charlotte. "Keith said you were doing a tour today, so I dropped my bags off then rushed over here to help. What do we need to do before the tour? We've got" —Brionna glanced at her watch— "sixty-seven minutes until it starts. But people will arrive a few minutes early, of course, so I think we'd better try to finish everything up in fifty minutes or less."

"Charlotte's been brilliant," Adam said, trying to reassure her with his eyes. "There really isn't much left to do before the tour. She's got everything under control."

Brionna grasped Charlotte's hand, giving it a squeeze. "That's music to my ears. I knew bringing you on was the right thing to do. I heard that the open house was a huge hit."

"I think it went well," Charlotte said. Her words were polite, but Adam recognized the dangerous undertones there.

"I'm sure today will be just as successful," Brionna said. "But first, we'd better get this place cleaned up. We've only got" —she glanced again at her watch— "sixty-six minutes until the tour begins, and this place is nowhere near ready for it."

Chapter Twenty-Two

The tour was going off without a hitch. But Charlotte couldn't enjoy it, because Brionna was getting on her last nerve. Little Miss Perfect had a way of stepping into any situation and instantly taking charge. It was only the years of decorum lessons with Mrs. Grant that prevented Charlotte from boldly taking back control. Her jaw ached from all the clenching.

Adam kept sending Charlotte furtive glances as Brionna directed the tour. Charlotte waited for him to step in and smoothly take over things himself, but he never did. And she didn't like it at all.

Charlotte knew that Adam hadn't known Brionna was coming back early. The shock on his face when she walked into the room had been enough to convince her of that much, at least. But why didn't he stand up to

Brionna—say that he and Charlotte appreciated the help but really didn't need it at the moment?

Her blood continued to boil as Brionna showed the council members around the small storeroom where school supplies would be kept for the children. Everything from pencils to tablets would be available for the students' use, all free of charge. That had been Charlotte's idea—one that she was funding personally. The students couldn't succeed without the proper tools, and Charlotte was happy to provide them.

She pressed her hands to her stomach, reminding herself that it wouldn't do to interrupt Brionna right now and make a scene. The important thing was that the children would get an exceptional education, which would in turn benefit the tribe for generations to come. It didn't matter who made that possible.

At least the tour was going well, even if Brionna was the one leading it. Charlotte watched the faces of the council members for any hint of hesitation or distrust, but they seemed excited about the progress that had been made on the building. Sure, some appeared more enthusiastic than others, but all the questions were respectful and there had been no outbursts or tense moments. If some of the members didn't seem thrilled, they at least no longer seemed outright hostile, which Charlotte counted as progress.

Adam stood beside Brionna, remaining mostly silent unless asked a direct question. Why was he letting Brionna walk all over him?

Brionna led them back into the front entryway and clasped her hands together. "Well, I think that's about it. Thank you so much for coming today and joining us in this venture."

Polite clapping filled the room, and then the delegates began to leave in little groups. Charlotte stood there, smiling at the council members and accepting their thanks. For once in her life, she hoped her feelings weren't plastered all over her face. It took a lot of effort to keep her hands relaxed at her sides instead of clenched into fists.

If she had a book right now, she might throw it at Brionna. After a week of fifteen-hour days spent prepping, the tour was over and she and Adam had barely said a word. Brionna had swooped in at the last moment and completely taken over.

As the front door swung shut behind the last of the council members, Chief Mandla walked over to their little group. He wore a suit and tie today instead of the traditional African robes Charlotte had seen him in at the open house, and his expression was grim.

Adam and Brionna stepped closer to Charlotte, the four of them forming a tight circle. Joseph and Karla stood a few paces away, and the sound of nail guns and the heavy bass of a rap song echoed from the second floor, but otherwise they were alone.

"I think that went well," Brionna said.

Charlotte folded her arms, biting her tongue so she wouldn't say something she'd later regret. Of course Brionna had thought it went well. She'd stepped in at the last moment and taken credit for Charlotte and Adam's hard work.

But the chief shook his head, his voice grave. "All is not as it appears."

Charlotte's stomach dropped to her toes as the world momentarily dimmed before coming sharply back into focus. Adam's face paled and his jaw clenched tightly.

"Are some of the council members still unhappy?" Charlotte asked, forcing the words past a tight throat. "Today they all appeared to be supportive of the school."

"It's not the council members," Chief Mandla said. "I will meet with them tonight to confirm, but I think you are right that they enjoyed the tour today. We seem to have finally convinced them that the school is a good thing. But it isn't just the council that we have to convince."

Adam ran a hand over his jaw, and the dark circles underneath his eyes suddenly seemed more pronounced. "You think that it's the boys you spoke to me about a few weeks ago."

Boys. What boys? Charlotte quickly ran over their conversations this week, but she couldn't recall any mention of this.

"Yes, those boys," Chief Mandla said. "I spoke to them yesterday afternoon. They were quite vocally upset about the council's tour today. I fear they may yet try to cause problems."

Brionna brushed her dark hair behind one shoulder, cheeks tinged pink. "How old are these boys?"

"Not yet men," Chief Mandla said. "Most are in their fifteenth year, although there are a few older and a few younger. But don't be fooled by their youth. They are fiercely protective of our way of life and fear that your school will destroy it."

How much trouble could a few boys cause? Charlotte clasped her hands together as she remembered the destruction she'd witnessed on her first tour of the school. Had the boys done that?

Charlotte knew how to convince a council to support the school—she'd done exactly that. But she didn't know how to convince teenage boys to stop vandalizing the property.

"I'll tell the night guards to be especially vigilant," Adam said. The words were confident, but his face was still pale and it made Charlotte nervous. "Thank you for letting me know."

The chief nodded, looking around the building once more. "It's a good thing we're doing here. I'm happy the project is finally back on track."

"Me too," Adam said. "In fact, Her Highness has interviews with prospective staff members set up all next week. We're hoping to have everyone hired by the end of the month."

Charlotte darted a glance at Brionna, but the news didn't seem to have upset the woman. Hopefully she'd get the message that this was Charlotte's project now, and she and Adam didn't need any help.

"We should be able to open on September first, barring any major problems," Adam continued. "Let's hope we don't encounter any."

"That's good news," the chief said. "I'll be on alert and let you know if I hear anything else. We'll keep in touch."

They shook hands, and Adam led the chief to the door. When Adam returned, his shoulders were hunched with tension.

"That went well," he said sarcastically.

Brionna put her hands on her hips, frowning. "I thought you'd resolved the issues with the vandals. We really can't afford anymore setbacks right now, Adam."

As if Adam had called up the vandals and asked them to keep causing trouble. "The guards are already on high alert," Charlotte said. "Things have been quiet all week. We're doing the best we can."

Brionna sent Charlotte a quick smile, but something about it grated on Charlotte's nerves.

"My apologies, Your Highness," Brionna said. "Of course I didn't mean to insult you. We're just on such a tight deadline, and the vandalism caused so many issues before."

"There's really nothing more we can do," Adam said.

"I disagree." Brionna pulled her phone from a small clutch and began typing into it. "I'll see if the guards can come in a half hour earlier tonight so we can discuss the situation with them."

Charlotte took a deep breath and counted to three in her head to keep from saying something she'd later regret. "I don't think that's necessary. Adam's already spoken to the guards numerous times, and they're aware of our concerns."

"It never hurts to double check . . ." Brionna trailed off, her words becoming incoherent mutters as she continued to focus on her phone's screen.

Charlotte stared hard at Adam, raising her eyebrows in what she hoped was a *well?* expression. But Adam just lifted his shoulders in a helpless shrug, causing Charlotte's temperature to rise another few degrees. Why wasn't he stepping in and being more assertive?

"There." Brionna pressed a button on her phone, turning the screen to black, then held it loosely in one hand. "That's done then. I'll start a list of specifics to discuss—"

Her words were cut off by a shrill ring. She glanced at her phone, then frowned. The display lit up with an incoming call, although Charlotte stood too far away to make out the name.

"Sorry, it's my brother," Brionna said. "Excuse me for a moment."

Charlotte would happily excuse Brionna for the rest of all eternity if it meant the woman would go away.

"Of course," Adam said. "Take your time."

"Thanks." Brionna walked a few paces away, turning her back for privacy.

Adam took a step closer to Charlotte, their shoulders nearly touching. When he spoke, his voice was a low murmur. "I'm so sorry about the tour. I didn't know how to put Bri in her place without causing a scene."

Charlotte folded her arms, the anger still coursing through her. His use of Brionna's nickname hadn't helped. "She wants you, Adam. That's what this is about."

Adam scratched the back of his head, but his cheeks were suspiciously pink. "You know it isn't like that between me and Brionna."

"No, I don't," Charlotte hissed. Every stolen kiss from the past week flashed through her mind. She thought of Brionna trapping Adam in some dark corner and kissing him the way Charlotte had kissed him, and her stomach churned until she worried she'd be sick all over the plywood floor. "And I don't think Brionna knows it isn't like that between the two of you, either."

"I'm going to tell her about us." Adam's lips brushed Charlotte's ear as he spoke. The length of his arm was pressed against the length of hers, sending bursts of fire through her body until she couldn't think. "I love you. Please tell me you believe that."

He loved her. Some of the nervous energy abated at those words. Charlotte was getting lost in his eyes again. It took a lot of effort not to throw herself at him.

"What?" Brionna said, her voice echoing across the room.

Charlotte and Adam sprang apart. Brionna had turned to face them, and for one panicked moment, Charlotte thought she'd seen the two of them and guessed at their relationship. But Brionna's eyes were unfocused. One hand was shoved roughly into her hair, and her face had gone ashen.

"No," Brionna moaned, the phone still pressed firmly to her ear. "Please, no."

Brionna swayed on her feet, and Adam jumped forward to catch her. He placed a steadying arm around Brionna's waist, but she barely seemed to notice. Charlotte's frustration with the woman vanished, replaced with concern. Something was very, very wrong. This went beyond Charlotte and Adam's secret relationship.

"What happened?" Adam demanded, giving Brionna a gentle shake. Whoever was on the other end of the line kept talking. Charlotte could just make out the deep intonations that indicated the caller was a man.

"It's my dad," Brionna whispered. "He's had a heart attack."

Chapter Twenty-Three

$\mathcal{B}$rionna's father had just had a heart attack. The African sun beat down harshly on Adam's back as he guided her down the front steps of the school and to the waiting car. Charlotte was on Brionna's other side, her brow pinched with concern.

Adam held open the car door, and Brionna climbed inside without a word.

A heart attack.

No one spoke until they were racing down the newly paved road toward the hotel. Brionna sat in the center seat, sandwiched between Charlotte and Adam, while Joseph occupied the front passenger seat. The setup was more squished than usual, but no one seemed to care. Adam certainly wasn't worried about it.

They were nearly back to the hotel when Charlotte finally broke the silence. "Did the doctors say anything about his prognosis?" she asked Brionna softly.

Brionna's face was as white as an elephant's tusks, her eyes red and luminescent with unshed tears. Visions of his mother's own illness swarmed in Adam's head. He focused once more on the road, feeling sick.

"Hudson wasn't sure of much. He'd just gotten the call from Dad's secretary and was on his way to the airport." Brionna squeezed her eyes shut tight. "No one is even with Dad in Boston right now. They're rushing him into emergency surgery, and it'll be hours before any of us can arrive."

Adam had been far from family when he learned of his mother's prognosis, too—half a world away in Mexico and unaware there was even cause for concern. Mother hadn't wanted to keep the truth from him, once the tests came back conclusively.

He couldn't just sit here and do nothing. Adam pulled out his phone, scrolling through his contacts. "I'll call the airstrip and have them prep the jet for departure."

Someone picked up on the other end of the line, and Adam quickly relayed instructions. He didn't dare look at Charlotte. Surely she wouldn't fault him for helping Brionna get to Boston as quickly as possible. She needed to be with her father right now, especially if the surgery . . .

Adam swallowed hard, putting the phone back in his pocket. Time had stood still in that hospital waiting room. His mother had ultimately undergone surgery three times. It had never gotten easier.

"I've already texted my secretary," Charlotte said, her tone as soft and soothing as ever. "We'll help you pack so you can be on your way as soon as possible."

Adam quickly glanced over, but Charlotte wasn't looking at him. She'd angled her body toward Brionna's, and Charlotte's eyes were hooded with concern. Her entire focus seemed to be Brionna.

Maybe Charlotte would understand why he'd ordered his private jet to take Brionna back to Boston. Adam felt the bands around his chest loosen. Of course Charlotte would understand. At the end of the day, Brionna was still a dear family friend, and right now her family was in crisis.

Adam wanted to crush Charlotte to him in a hug. Whisper in her ear how much he appreciated her compassion and understanding.

The car pulled to a stop, and Charlotte's secretary met them at the sliding glass doors. Adam hung back, sticking to Brionna's side. Her eyes were glassy, and she barely seemed aware of her surroundings.

"Your Highness," Charlotte's secretary said, falling into step beside the princess. "I contacted the hotel staff, and they sent maids up to begin packing Miss

Cartwright's belongings. I also took the liberty of creating a basic packing list so that nothing is forgotten in the rush."

"Thank you, Becky," Charlotte said. She glanced over her shoulder at Adam. "How long until the jet is ready to leave?"

"Just as soon as we can get there," Adam said, glancing again at Brionna. She clutched her cell phone as if it were a lifeline, but Adam knew it would probably be hours before she got another update.

Brionna's suite was a flutter of activity as maids bustled about, trying to pack all of her things. Adam watched in amazement as Charlotte took charge, efficiently managing the chaos. Brionna sat on her bed, barely answering Charlotte's questions and making no move to pack herself.

Adam knew that Brionna's future would hold long days—maybe weeks—spent at the hospital as she oversaw every aspect of her father's recovery. If he recovered. Adam had spent long days and even longer nights in those uncomfortable plastic-covered hospital chairs, watching his mother's cheeks grow more and more hollow. He could almost smell the antiseptic, even now.

But he'd at least known that death was coming. Adam had been gifted three years to prepare, and a chance to say goodbye. He couldn't imagine how

Brionna would get through this if her father passed before she could do the same.

"I think we're nearly done here, Your Highness," Becky said. "If you'll give us just a few more min—"

Brionna's phone rang, and the entire room fell silent. Adam tensed as Brionna pressed the phone to her ear, watching her face for a clue as to what kind of news she was receiving on the other end of the line. But Brionna barely said a handful of words and hung up only a minute or so later.

"Is everything okay?" Charlotte asked, her tone cautious. Adam was glad she'd posed the question, because his mouth felt full of cotton.

"I don't know." Brionna ran a shaky hand through her hair. "It wasn't the hospital. Hudson just wanted to let me know he's boarded the plane in California. It's a direct flight, so he should be at the hospital in only a few hours. Mason is in Thailand, and Ethan's in Australia. I'm not sure which of the three of us will get there next."

Charlotte waved her hand, and the maids jumped back into action. "We'll leave for the airstrip in ten minutes. With a little luck and a good tail wind, you should arrive just a few hours after Hudson."

Adam pulled out his phone once more. "I'll let the pilot know we're on our way so there aren't any delays at the airstrip."

Brionna's eyes grew panicked, and she stumbled to her feet. Her hand clamped around Adam's upper arm like a vice. "You're coming with me, aren't you?"

Coming with her? Adam coughed into his fist, panic making him dizzy.

He couldn't go to a hospital. Couldn't leave Charlotte to deal with the school while he went to Boston with Brionna. "I'm not sure—"

"Of course he's going with you," Charlotte cut in.

Adam coughed again. Had the stress of the situation made him fall asleep? Because surely this was a dream. Charlotte wouldn't suggest he go to Boston.

Brionna dropped her hand from Adam's arm. Her shoulders sagged, relief evident in her expression. Charlotte's own face was unreadable, and Adam wondered what she was thinking.

Was Charlotte mad he'd offered the jet for Brionna's use? Did she think he wanted to be with Brionna instead of her?

"Thank you," Brionna breathed. "I need you right now, Adam. There's so much to do. I'm sure that it'll be months before Daddy can go back to work, and I have no idea where to start with the company. If he ever goes back." She pressed her fingers to her lips, blinking rapidly. "He's always kept such a tight control on things. I bet even his personal assistant is unaware of everything that will need to be done. I'll have to try to figure it out so the business doesn't suffer while he's in recovery."

Adam cleared his throat, feeling uneasy. He still couldn't get a read on Charlotte. Why had she suggested he go with Brionna? "I'll go pack then. You'd better give me fifteen minutes, instead of ten."

Brionna nodded. Instead of sinking back down to the edge of the bed, she moved to the suitcase a maid was packing and began rifling through the contents.

"May I have a word with you, Your Highness?" Adam asked pointedly. "There are a few things we should discuss about the school before I leave."

"Of course," Charlotte said. She motioned to Becky. "See that this is finished up. I'll meet you in the lobby in fifteen minutes."

Becky nodded, and Charlotte followed Adam from the room. He shut the door to Brionna's suite firmly behind them and turned to face Charlotte.

"What are you doing?" he hissed. "We've got so much to do on the school right now. Are you upset with me or something? I had to offer her the plane, Char. She needs—"

"Shh." Charlotte pressed a soft finger to Adam's lips, stealing his breath and his focus. He loved the way she always smelled faintly of vanilla. Right now, what he really wanted to do was push her up against the door and ravage her mouth with his. Forget Boston.

253

Charlotte dropped her hand, and Adam shook his head to clear the cobwebs from it.

"Brionna can't fly to Boston alone," Charlotte said. "It would be cruel to send her on a nineteen-hour flight with zero emotional support. Right now, she needs you more than I do."

The truth of the words hit Adam, and he felt himself falling in love with Charlotte all over again. Brionna was supposed to be his friend, and yet Charlotte was the one encouraging him to do the right thing. He took her hands, pressing a gentle kiss to the tip of each finger. "I don't want to leave you."

Her eyes softened, and she rose on tip-toes and brushed a soft kiss across his lips. "You'll only be gone a few days, and I can handle things with the school for that long. Once Brionna's with her brothers, you can come home."

Charlotte was right. Brionna did need someone to go with her to Boston, and it had to be him. Maybe he and Brionna would never be the married couple his mother had envisioned, but they were still friends.

Adam pulled Charlotte to him, wrapping her in a hug. She rested her head on his chest with a gentle sigh, and Adam kissed the crown of her head.

"Three days," he said. "It'll really only be one day without seeing each other, if you think about it. I'll fly out with Brionna tonight, then leave as soon as her brothers arrive."

Charlotte nodded. "Keep me updated on how Mr. Cartwright is doing."

"Definitely. I'll text you constantly." Adam leaned down, brushing his lips slowly across hers. "I'm going to miss you very much, Your Highness."

"Then hurry back to me."

"I will."

Chapter Twenty-Four

It had been twenty-two hours since Adam had last held Charlotte in his arms. Twenty-two long, exhausting, lonely hours. He missed her with an intensity he hadn't known was possible and longed to be back in South Africa. But more and more, it was looking like his quick trip to Boston might last longer than he'd anticipated.

Brionna had been an emotional mess during the nineteen-hour flight, and neither of them had gotten much sleep. Mr. Cartwright had made it through the surgery, but just barely. They'd only been at the hospital three hours, and his condition had already worsened significantly in that amount of time. Adam didn't like the look in the doctors' eyes. Each solemn expression hinted that the prognosis wasn't encouraging.

Adam leaned his head back against the wall and closed his eyes, hating the gritty sandpaper feel that reminded him too much of the long days spent at the hospital during his mother's illness. At least he was alone in the waiting room for the moment instead of sharing an uncomfortable silence with strangers. A TV was mounted on the far wall, the volume turned low as the laugh track from some sitcom filled the space.

He shifted, making the plastic on the chairs squeak as he tried to find a more comfortable position. Adam doubted he'd slept more than thirty minutes since leaving South Africa. The few snatches of rest he'd managed to catch while Brionna was in with her father hadn't done much for his exhaustion.

Since Mr. Cartwright wasn't stable, Brionna and Hudson were only allowed to spend fifteen minutes of every hour at their father's side. They spent the other forty-five minutes in the ICU waiting room with Adam, where he tried his best to comfort and distract the Cartwright siblings from their father's condition.

Ethan and Mason's planes had both landed, and the brothers should arrive at the hospital within the hour. But Adam wasn't sure how he could leave the four siblings to deal with everything alone. The memories of his own mother's illness were still so fresh. He knew the fog that filled their brains, making it hard to think, let alone make a decision, because he'd experienced it, too.

His phone buzzed, the screen lighting up with a text from Charlotte.

Any change?

No, Adam quickly texted back. **How are things with the school?**

Everything is going well. You'll be home soon enough to look after things. We can manage just fine without you for a day or two.

A day or two. How was Adam going to tell Charlotte he wasn't sure he could leave tomorrow?

Brionna walked in just then, and Adam was shocked once again by her appearance. Her eyes were red-rimmed, navy blue dress wrinkled, and her hair was pulled back in some sort of messy braid.

Adam swallowed hard and quickly rose, shoving his phone back in his pocket. He'd never seen her so completely undone. Brionna was always composed. Even as children, she'd been so in control of her emotions. Adam had often teased her about it.

"How is he?" Adam asked.

Brionna stumbled across the room, falling into Adam. He instinctively pulled her to him in a hug, shocked to feel her body trembling.

"Did something happen?" Adam asked, feeling suddenly panicked. "Where is Hudson?"

"I told him to go grab us something to eat." Brionna sniffed, still not letting go of Adam. The hug was beginning to feel a little uncomfortable. "My father looks so frail, Adam. I've never seen him so weak."

"Is he still unconscious?"

Brionna finally pulled back, but surprised Adam by taking his hand and tugging back down into a chair. She sat down beside him, not letting go of his hand.

Adam's discomfort skyrocketed, and he swallowed uncomfortably. Should he pull away? Brionna wasn't a touchy-feely person, and they'd never had that kind of relationship. But maybe she needed the human contact right now to keep her grounded. Adam could relate to that. He'd felt like a ship adrift at sea, desperate for any anchor he could find.

"The doctors aren't sure he'll ever wake up," Brionna said, her voice barely a whisper.

"Oh, Bri. Has he taken a turn for the worse?"

"His vitals aren't where they'd like them to be. I don't know." Brionna wiped underneath her eyes with her free hand, still not letting go of Adam's. "I just don't know what to do. How am I supposed to take over Cartwright Industries? Best-case scenario, it'll be months before he can return to work."

Adam patted Brionna's hand, resisting the urge to pull away. He wanted to be her friend. To help her through this difficult time.

But he also loved Charlotte. And he was beginning to think she'd been right about what Brionna really wanted—him.

260

"The business should be the least of your worries right now," Adam said. "But you will fill whatever role is required of you flawlessly. I've never met someone with such a head for business."

Her eyes filled with tears, and she scooted forward, angling her body toward his until their knees touched. She still hadn't let go of his hand, and the laugh track for the sitcom playing on the TV in the corner of the room suddenly seemed loud and grating.

"I know I can do anything with you here supporting me." Brionna rested her free hand on top of his, creating an awkward hand-holding sandwich he wasn't sure how to escape. "Thank you again for coming. Just knowing you're here with me is the best comfort I could ask for right now."

Oh boy. Adam gently removed his hand from in between Brionna's, then loosened his tie. It felt like a noose right now, and he was desperate for air.

"I'm happy to help you—as a friend." Adam searched her eyes, hoping his meaning was clear.

Brionna sat back, folding her arms. Her eyes darkened, instantly guarded. "As a friend?"

Adam nodded. "And only a friend."

"I'm such an idiot." She ran a hand through her hair, pulling apart her messy braid and causing it to hang in tangles about her shoulders. "It's Princess Charlotte, isn't it?"

The pain in Brionna's eyes was so strong that Adam could practically taste it. But he forced himself to be honest—for both of their sakes—and nodded. "I'm sorry I didn't tell you about it sooner. We dated briefly when I was in Durham and reconnected when she came to South Africa for the education conference."

"I thought there might be something between you. I mean, the chemistry was obvious to anyone with eyes." Brionna gave a hollow laugh. "I guess I was fooling myself to think that you and I had some sort of unspoken agreement."

His mother's carefully constructed plans for Adam's imaginary future with Brionna once again forced their way into the forefront of his thoughts, but Adam pushed them back. He loved Charlotte. And he wasn't about to deny that. "I thought I was over Charlotte after Durham, but I was wrong."

"Do you love her?"

Adam nodded. "I do. I'm sorry, Bri."

"And I thought today couldn't possibly get any worse," Brionna murmured.

"I'm sorry," Adam repeated. "I do care about you, Brionna, but it can only ever be as a friend."

She rose, hands on hips, and glared down at him with eyes fierce with determination. Adam scooted back in his seat, shocked by this sudden switch from weepy to steely.

"What you and I have has never been about romantic love, Adam. But we make such a great team together. We're partners in the truest sense of the word. Look at what we've been able to accomplish with the school. That project was nearly dead in the water, but together we managed to hold things together."

Adam slowly rose as well, wanting to refute her claims but knowing now wasn't the time. Brionna had stepped in, unasked, and taken charge. But Adam had let her, and that was on him. She had helped keep the school afloat until Charlotte stepped in, and he'd forever be grateful to Brionna for that. "We do make a good team, and I respect you so much. But I love Charlotte. I'm sorry, Bri."

"No." Brionna shook her head, holding up both hands as she backed away from Adam. "This isn't how things are supposed to play out. We're supposed to get married. Merge the companies and run them together. Everyone expects it to happen. Your mother, your father, my father . . ."

Her voice caught on the last word, tears welling in her eyes, but Adam was still reeling from the punch she'd unexpectedly thrown.

Brionna had known his mother wanted them to end up together. Had the two women spoken about him? Brionna had always been close to his mother, especially after the death of her own mother and abandonment of her step-mother.

"I'll stay here as long as you need me to," Adam said. "I know how stressful this is, and I'm happy to help in whatever way I can. But only as a friend."

"You'll never be Charlotte's equal."

The words sliced through Adam like a whip, stealing his breath. But Brionna wasn't done.

"She's a princess, for heaven's sake. Do you think the royal family will allow you to continue running the Hotel Montgomery if you marry her? You'll be Charlotte's lap dog, at her beck and call."

He felt frozen, unable to move. Unable to speak.

Brionna took a step forward, as though sensing she'd found a weakness. "Charlotte will destroy you, Adam. Joining the royal family will cage your soul. All of your hopes, all of your dreams—everything you've spent a lifetime building—will disappear just like that." She snapped her fingers, the sound reverberating in Adam's ears. "Is that what you want?"

"Charlotte wouldn't do that to me." But suddenly he wasn't so certain. Would she really have a choice? Royalty didn't make accommodations for anyone or anything.

"She's already doing it. We belong together. When are you going to realize that?"

Adam could hear his every heartbeat, and wondered if Brionna could, too. Was she right about Charlotte? Had his mother known that Brionna was what Adam needed in his life?

Hudson skidded into the room, breaking the silence. His light brown hair stood on end, and his eyes were wild.

"He's coding again," Hudson said, his words tumbling over each other. "You'd better come quick."

Brionna glanced at Adam, who waved his hands quickly in a *go* motion. Brionna gave a sharp nod, and raced out of the room after Hudson.

Adam sank back into the chair, feeling as though his entire world had imploded. He pulled out his phone again.

I miss you, Charlotte had texted. **Hurry back soon.**

Should he tell Charlotte about the conversation with Brionna? It would probably freak Charlotte out, and Brionna didn't know what she was saying. Her father was sick, possibly dying, and she held the weight of the world on her shoulders right now. Adam knew what that felt like. He'd hate to be held accountable for the stupid things he'd probably said and done in his grief.

Brionna didn't really want Adam. She was just scared of all the changes and didn't want to lose yet another constant in her life.

Slowly, Adam typed out a reply. **Mr. Cartwright just took another turn for the worse. I'm not sure how long until I can come home.**

He couldn't go back to South Africa. Not right now.

Adam bowed his head and began to pray for Mr. Cartwright, and the doctors that were currently trying to save his life.

Chapter Twenty-Five

Charlotte tossed her phone onto the coffee table, anger making her hands tremble. The phone skidded across the polished black surface, then teetered on the edge for a moment before tumbling to the plush cheetah-print rug beneath the table.

It was nearly eleven o'clock—way past when she wanted to be in bed—and Charlotte was exhausted from another long day spent at the school. The wrong flooring had showed up today—a horrifyingly orange-toned hardwood floor—and the company couldn't seem to locate where the right flooring had been shipped. They claimed it would take another two weeks to get the correct product to the school, and that was time Charlotte didn't have. She'd spent all day talking to the contractor, but he wasn't sure that sanding down and re-staining the flooring they had could be done any quicker.

Charlotte hadn't heard much from Adam, but she had tried to calm her worries. Mr. Cartwright wasn't doing well. He'd coded twice during the night, and the doctors were worried his heart wouldn't survive a third code. Adam was probably busy helping Brionna with the business side of things while she stayed at the hospital.

After returning to her suite for the night, Charlotte had sunk onto the couch and pulled out her phone for some mindless web surfing to try to distract herself. That's when she'd found the article.

The paparazzi, sharks that they were, had somehow found out not only about Mr. Cartwright's illness, but that Adam was at the hospital with Brionna. Words like *new relationship* and *one bright spot in the midst of tragedy* were being used. It set Charlotte's teeth on edge and made her feel like a fraud.

She knew how the paparazzi, and reporters in general, could twist the truth. They truly had a gift for taking small, innocent moments and blowing them out of proportion. Hadn't her brothers taught her that much at least?

Outright lies had been told about Alex's breakup with that slimy actress, Isla Martin. Later, Alex had purposefully used the press to circulate news of his fake relationship with Libby. And true, they'd eventually fallen in love and were now happily married—at least Charlotte assumed they were enjoying their honeymoon—but the point was that the press lied all the time.

Henry was constantly being linked in the press with various super models and celebrities, and Charlotte knew that those reports were generally false as well. So why was it so hard to believe the gossip websites were once again lying, but this time about Adam and Brionna?

Charlotte leaned down with a groan and picked up her cell phone. Thankfully, the fall hadn't cracked the screen, and she opened up the article once again.

The photo was grainy, but Charlotte would recognize Adam anywhere. He and Brionna were holding hands as they walked into some building that was probably the hospital.

Maybe Brionna had tripped on the curb, and Adam was holding her hand to steady her. Or perhaps Boston was experiencing an uncharacteristic summer cold front, and it was necessary for Brionna and Adam to hold hands for warmth.

Or maybe Adam had decided a relationship with a princess was too much, and he'd rather be with the hotel heiress. The two of them had a lot in common. A relationship with Brionna made a lot more sense on paper than a relationship with Charlotte, and she knew the Cartwrights and Montgomerys had always been close.

Charlotte gulped, holding the phone to her chest. Why couldn't she trust Adam completely? He'd broken her heart in Durham, sure, but that had been before he said he loved her.

The phone rang, and Charlotte quickly checked the screen. Adam! She fumbled to answer the phone, pressing it tightly to her ear. "Hello?"

"Sorry to call so late. Did I wake you?"

Charlotte closed her eyes, the low rumble of Adam's voice bringing tears to her eyes. She missed him so much.

"No, I'm still awake. How is Mr. Cartwright doing?"

"I don't know if he's going to make it. They think he had another heart attack today. Just a minor one, but he's already so weak."

Charlotte tightened her grip on the phone as she heard Adam sigh across the line.

"I'm so sorry." Charlotte swallowed hard, forcing herself to push aside her jealousy. She was running herself into the ground trying to keep the school project on schedule while Adam kept extending his trip. "How is Brionna handling it?"

"I've never seen her so unhinged. I thought maybe she'd calm down once Mason and Ethan arrived, but she's an emotional mess. Not surprising, considering the circumstances."

"Not at all surprising," Charlotte agreed. She didn't want to even think about how she'd handle things if the situations were reversed.

"Don't be mad, Char."

She squeezed her eyes tightly shut, feeling the hot burn of suppressed tears. She knew where this conversation was going.

"You're staying in Boston for a few more days," she said flatly.

"I'm sorry. I can't leave them to deal with this alone."

But he had no problem leaving her alone to deal with the school. She hadn't had a chance to tell him about the flooring mix-up, but he knew what a time crunch they were on. It was all hands on deck, and yet the boss was conspicuously missing. Was it because he'd changed his mind about her?

Last time, she hadn't asked Adam outright where their relationship stood and instead had spent months living with *what if*s. She refused to make the same mistake again.

"Do you . . . do you have feelings for Brionna, Adam?"

Silence stretched across the line for so long that Charlotte wondered if the call had dropped. She pulled back the phone to check, but Adam hadn't hung up.

"Adam?" Charlotte ventured.

"Why would you ask me that?" His voice sounded wounded, like she'd deeply hurt him.

Charlotte sighed, dropping her head back against the couch cushions. A headache throbbed at her temples, threatening to explode into a full-blown migraine at the slightest provocation. "I'm sorry. One of the gossip sites had a photo of you and Brionna holding hands, and it messed with my head."

"You know better than to listen to the rags. They tell more lies than a politician on a reelection campaign."

Not exactly the reassurance Charlotte wanted. "So you don't love Brionna?"

"Of course not. I love you, Char. Even when we're half a world apart. Do you think I want to still be here? But I don't know what else to do."

The honesty in his voice brought tears to Charlotte's eyes, and she brushed them aside. She grabbed one of the throw pillows and curled it against her stomach, suddenly feeling desperately alone. "I love you, too. And I miss you. Sorry. It's been a stressful day."

"Want to tell me about it?"

She hugged the pillow tighter, feeling her attitude soften. "Yeah. There was a mix-up with the flooring, and—"

Muffled voices sounded on the other end of the line, and Adam broke in. "Char, I'm really sorry, but Hudson just got here. Can we talk about this later?"

"Oh." She sank into the couch cushions like a deflated balloon. "Yeah, sure."

"You're the best. I'll be home before you know it. Bye."

"Bye," Charlotte said. But Adam had already hung up.

Charlotte stared at the phone, fighting the urge to cry. She'd told Adam to go to Boston with Brionna. But she'd also asked him to come home as soon as Ethan and Mason arrived.

She pulled up her texts, staring at the four unanswered ones from Emma. Her cousin had been less than thrilled to learn of Adam's absence and was lukewarm at best toward Charlotte's new relationship. Consequently, Charlotte had been dodging Emma's calls and texts.

Charlotte hesitated, then typed out a quick text. **Are you still awake?**

A moment later, the phone rang. Charlotte sighed, regretting her rash action. She shouldn't have texted Emma. Now if she didn't answer, Emma would know she was avoiding her.

"Hey," Charlotte said, then winced at the false brightness in her tone. She'd laid it on too thick, and Emma would notice.

"Is everything okay?" Emma asked immediately.

Charlotte rubbed her eyes, the headache kicking up a notch at the question. "Yeah, of course. They finished painting today. We're supposed to start installing the flooring next week, but they sent the wrong order. I'll get it sorted out, though."

"That's all?"

"I'm hoping we can hire a principal soon. Becky's got all of the interviews set up and I'm meeting with the first candidate tomorrow."

"That's not what I meant," Emma said. Now her voice was soothing, like she was speaking to a wounded animal. It made Charlotte feel even worse. "Is Adam still in Boston?"

Charlotte clutched the pillow tighter to her stomach, feeling sick. "Mr. Cartwright is really ill—"

"And there are doctors doing the best they can to help him," Emma cut in. "Char, don't you see how messed up this is? Sure, Brionna is a family friend. But he's been in Boston for four days now."

"I'm the one who told him to go with her."

"Yeah, and he was supposed to be home yesterday. How much longer is he going to stay with her, when you need his help with the school?"

Now Emma was just making Charlotte mad. She rose, heading toward her bedroom. Time to put an end to this conversation and go to bed, because her headache wasn't getting any better. "I'm handling things with the school just fine. The flooring is a setback, but I'm on it. Don't make me out to be some damsel in distress."

"That's not the point, and you know it. This is *his* project, Char. And he's leaving his secret girlfriend to deal with the mess while he comforts the mistress in Boston."

"Don't say that." Charlotte slammed her bedroom door shut and yanked off her shirt with one hand, then pulled her pajamas from the closet. "He's being a good friend."

"He's being a bad boyfriend," Emma countered. "At some point, he's going to have to make a choice and decide which is more important."

"I have to go," Charlotte said.

"Char—"

She hung up, cutting off Emma mid-sentence. Charlotte finished getting ready for bed, anger making her movements jerky, then slipped between the sheets.

Emma was wrong. Adam wasn't abandoning Charlotte—he was helping Brionna. What was he supposed to do, leave her to deal with her father's illness alone?

Except she wasn't alone. She had three brothers at the hospital, helping each other through this difficult time. And hadn't Brionna grown up in Boston? Surely she had friends somewhere in the city.

"He loves me," Charlotte said aloud.

But Emma's words wouldn't leave Charlotte, and it was a very long time before she finally drifted off into an uneasy slumber.

Chapter Twenty-Six

Adam yawned, checking the time on his watch. It was nearly mid-morning, but he'd spent another sleepless night in the ICU waiting room.

He glanced at the empty doorway, then at the pot of coffee waiting on the sideboard. It was tempting to make himself another cup, even if the taste left a lot to be desired. But he reluctantly took a sip of water and turned back to his computer. Charlotte had sent him a summary of the applicants she'd scheduled interviews with and promised to let him know her thoughts after she met with each candidate. The first interview should be sometime today. Or had it already happened? He couldn't seem to keep track of the time difference.

Brionna stumbled through the doorway, her heel catching on the trim with a loud clang. Her hair hung limply around her face and her eyes were wild with fear. Hudson, Mason, and Ethan were right behind her.

Adam quickly shut his laptop lid and rose. "What's wrong?" he asked urgently.

But he already knew what was wrong. It was written all over Brionna's face.

"Another massive heart attack." She swallowed hard. "They tried to revive him, but they couldn't. Adam . . . He didn't make it."

Mr. Cartwright was dead. Brionna was an orphan.

Her entire world had just collapsed.

"Oh, Bri." Adam held out his arms, and she collapsed into them.

Hudson ran a hand through his hair, making the light brown locks stand on end.

"The doctor said his heart was too weak from the previous attacks. And then there was the surgery, of course . . ."

"There was nothing they could do," Ethan—or maybe it was Mason? Adam still had a hard time telling the triplets apart—said.

Adam had heard those words before. They'd irreversibly changed his entire world.

Brionna buried her face in Adam's neck with a sob. He swallowed hard, pulling her close. There was a lump in his throat the size of Durham, and tears pricked at his eyes.

"I am so sorry," Adam whispered. "I am so, so sorry."

"How can he be gone?" Brionna asked. "I don't know what I'll do without him."

A wave of grief poured over Adam, surprising him with its intensity. While he'd spent a lot of time with the Cartwright siblings growing up, he hadn't known Mr. Cartwright well. The mothers had always taken care of the kids while the fathers worked.

But Adam knew intimately the pain Brionna and her brothers were now going through. And his heart broke for them.

Sniffs came from the direction of the triplets. Adam looked over Brionna's head at the trio. They were clustered together, arms around each other's shoulders and heads bowed close together.

But Brionna didn't go to her brothers. She clung to Adam, his shirt growing damp with her tears.

The embrace felt wrong somehow—too tight and too dependent. Shouldn't she turn to her brothers right now? As a friend, Adam longed to comfort her. But he thought of their conversation from a few days ago— one he still hadn't told Charlotte about—and wondered if the hug meant more to Brionna than it meant to him.

He carefully disentangled himself from Brionna, urging her into her brother's tight-knit circle. They enveloped her, and Adam tried to step away and give the family some space. But Brionna's hand lashed out, clamping around his wrist and tugging him back to her side.

Adam wasn't sure how long they stayed like that in the ICU waiting room—a few minutes? An hour? Time seemed to stand still as the family clung to each other, processing their grief. Adam felt like an intruder, but Brionna kept her arm firmly linked through Adam's, refusing to let him go.

Eventually Hudson suggested they head back to the hotel, and the others agreed. They climbed into the black limo waiting for them outside the hospital and rode silently through the streets of Boston toward the highrise that was the Cartwright Hotel.

The brothers murmured goodnight, disappearing into the presidential suite, but Brionna lingered in the hallway. Her cheeks were streaked with salt trails from the dried tears, and her voice was thick when she said, "I can't believe he's really dead."

Adam gave Brionna a side-hug, careful not to hold on for longer than was appropriate. He didn't want to send the wrong message.

"There is nothing I can say that will make you feel better right now," Adam said quietly. It was the middle of the night, and the hallway lights were dim. "But I really am so, so sorry, Brionna."

She brushed at her cheeks, and in that moment she looked completely lost and alone. "When will it stop hurting?"

Adam thought of his mother, his heart twinging with the loss. He wished so badly that he could call her on the phone and just talk. He wanted to tell her about Charlotte. About how incredibly happy she made him. About the progress he'd made with the school, and the intense and unexpected satisfaction that brought. Maybe, if he could talk to Mother, she would have gladly taken those blueprints for the Cartwright-Montgomery Hotel and tossed them in the trash.

"I'm not sure it ever does get easier," Adam said. "But you learn to live your life again. Right now, though, you need to give yourself time to grieve."

Brionna didn't say anything, and Adam gently guided her toward the suite door that was still open a crack.

"You should be with your brothers right now," Adam said. "I'll see you in the morning. Text me when you're awake. I don't want to disturb you."

Brionna nodded, and the door shut quietly behind her. Adam headed across the hallway to his own suite, letting himself inside with a sigh.

He slipped out of his shoes and loosened his tie, fighting the tears that wanted to flow out of him like a waterfall. This was so stupid. He hadn't known Mr.

Cartwright that well. Certain not well enough to feel this all-encompassing grief.

But these tears weren't for Mr. Cartwright. Tonight had been a painful reminder of Adam's own loss, and it tore him apart inside.

He fished out his phone and sank onto the edge of his bed. Charlotte had texted him a few hours ago—something about the first interview and how it had gone well. The words swam on the screen as his eyes blurred.

He swiped away the moisture and sent her a quick text. **Mr. Cartwright died a few hours ago.**

Adam waited, hoping Charlotte would text him back. He was desperate to hear her voice. She was such a great listener, and right now he could really use a sounding board. But a text never came through, and Adam set aside his phone.

It was late in South Africa. Charlotte was probably already asleep. She'd see the text in the morning.

He mustered the energy to slip from his suit into lounge pants and a loose-fitting T-shirt, then brushed his teeth and climbed into bed. But Adam was too keyed-up to fall asleep, and so he flipped on the television and settled on some mindless TV show about the world's most unique hotels.

He'd nearly drifted to sleep when a soft knock sounded at the doorway. Adam sat up in bed with a start, rubbing the sleep from his eyes. Had he imagined the noise?

The sound came again, a gentle *tap-tap-tap* on the suite's outer door.

Adam stumbled from his room and toward the door, peering through the peephole. Brionna.

He quickly undid the chain latch and opened the door. "Brionna. What's the matter—"

She threw herself at him, and suddenly Brionna's lips were pressed against his, too warm and too soft. Adam stumbled backward, but her arms were vices around his neck and he only managed to drag her back with him. The door swung shut behind her, the click echoing loudly in the stillness.

Adam tore his lips away from Brionna's, feeling his neck heat with anger.

"What are you doing?" he asked.

Her arms closed around his neck once more like octopus tentacles. Adam struggled to loosen her grip, but she clung to him.

"Why don't you want me, Adam?" she asked, her voice soft and pathetic. "We could be so good together. Give us a chance. We'll merge the companies and have a real empire on our hands."

Her lips moved toward his again. Adam quickly covered his mouth with one hand and Brionna's lips landed on his knuckles. Her eyes popped open, wide with surprise.

"I love Charlotte," he said. "I told you that."

Her grip finally did relax then, and Adam gently pushed Brionna away.

"You could love me, too, if you gave us a chance. We make so much more sense than you and Charlotte ever will."

"Bri, you aren't thinking clearly right now." Adam took another step backward, wanting to put as much distance between them as possible. "You're scared about the business, and that's understandable. But you don't need me. You don't even want me. Not really."

"I do." She leaned forward again, but Adam took another quick step back, putting the couch between them.

"I love Charlotte," he repeated.

The words bounced around in his brain as reality settled over him. What was he doing? He loved Charlotte, and yet he was here with Brionna. Panic shot through him as he imagined explaining this all to Charlotte. She'd warned him Brionna wanted more, but he'd brushed her fears aside.

He shouldn't be here. Not anymore. He should have left as soon as he'd seen Brionna safely into her brothers' care.

Yes, Charlotte was a princess. Loving her would change Adam's entire life. But wasn't that what love was supposed to do—alter your future for the better?

He didn't care that loving Charlotte meant destroying his mother's dream for Adam's future. He didn't care that marrying her might ruin his father's business merger plans. He didn't even care that marrying Charlotte would probably mean giving up the Hotel Montgomery. Because he loved her, and he wanted all of her. Forever.

Adam had to get back to South Africa.

"I'm sorry, Bri," Adam said. "But I have to go home."

"I can't do this without you." Brionna choked on the last word, her shoulders suddenly shaking with heaving sobs. "I need you, Adam. My brothers don't know the hotel business like you do. Cartwright Industries will collapse without your help."

"No, they won't." He took her firmly by the shoulders, making his voice steely. "You are Brionna Cartwright. You don't need anyone to help you make this company a success."

She crumbled against him, tears soaking his T-shirt, and Adam's heart ached for her.

Brionna wasn't here because of him. She was here because she thought he could help take away the pain of her father's loss. But nothing could do that. Time would dull the pain, but for now, she just had to live through it.

Adam carefully led Brionna from his room and down the hallway. For the first time, he realized she wore only a thin satin pajama set. The minuscule shorts and lacy tank top didn't leave much to the imagination, and he wished he'd thought to drape a blanket around her shoulders. Too late now.

Adam paused in front of her suite door. "Do you have your key?"

Brionna shook her head, sagging against him.

Adam nodded and rapped firmly on the door. A moment later, Hudson opened it, looking confused. He squinted against the dim light of the hallway, rubbing his eyes.

"Sorry to wake you," Adam said, keeping his voice low.

Hudson glanced back and forth between Adam and Brionna, as though just realizing what he was seeing. One eyebrow raised. "Uh, hi?"

Adam transferred Brionna into Hudson's arms, then took a step back to put some distance between them. Brionna collapsed against Hudson, burying her face in his shoulder.

"She came to my room, and . . . yeah." By the way Hudson's eyebrows shot up his forehead, Adam knew the younger man understood the implication. "I'm so sorry for your family's loss, Hudson. But it's past time for me to return to my girlfriend in South Africa."

"Girlfriend?" Hudson asked, glancing down at Brionna.

Adam nodded, feeling like a total cad. Would Brionna tell Hudson she'd known about Charlotte, or would Brionna claim Adam had led her on? Hopefully, a lifetime of childhood memories would convince Hudson of Adam's character. Not that it mattered—not really. The important thing was getting home to Charlotte.

"I'm sorry I didn't leave sooner," Adam said. "Please, if I can be of any help in any way during this difficult time, send me an email. But I think it's best I communicate with you or one of your brothers, at least for now."

Hudson nodded in understanding, and relief flowed through Adam. Hudson wouldn't blame him for tonight.

He held out a hand, giving Adam's a firm shake. "You're a good man, Montgomery. Thank you for everything."

Adam nodded, casting one more glance at Brionna. "Goodbye," he whispered.

She didn't look up, instead keeping her face buried against Hudson's chest. But Adam couldn't let his feelings about his mother's death keep him here any longer.

Brionna didn't need him—she needed her family. And Adam needed to be with Charlotte.

He stumbled to his room, anxious to find his phone and let the pilot know they were finally going home. After a five-minute search, Adam found his phone tangled in his bedsheets and quickly made the call. They'd leave for South Africa immediately.

Charlotte still hadn't replied to his text about Mr. Cartwright's death. Adam debated calling her, but didn't want to wake her if she was asleep. Instead, he packed up his bag as quickly as he could and then called for a car to take him to the airport.

He'd surprise Charlotte with his return. Hopefully, it would be a good surprise. She had every right to be upset with him right now, because Adam had definitely had his priorities all wrong the past few days. Maybe his entire life.

But Adam knew what he wanted now. He wanted Charlotte. And he wasn't about to let anything else get in the way.

He grabbed his suitcase and headed out the door, letting it swing firmly shut behind him.

He was going home.

Chapter Twenty-Seven

The phone rang loudly in the still room, and Charlotte sat straight up in bed, grabbing for her cell.

"Hello?" she said.

"Your Highness, come quickly. There's a fire at the school." Even in her half-awake state, she recognized the deep voice as belonging to one of the night guards at the school.

Charlotte shot out of bed, already fumbling for the closest pair of clothes. "Have you called the fire department?"

"Yes, Your Highness."

"I'm on my way." Charlotte hung up the phone and dropped it onto her bed, quickly changing into the pair of comfortable slacks and the loose blouse she'd grabbed.

A knock sounded at the door, and Charlotte knew it was either Karla or Joseph. "Come in."

Karla cautiously entered the room, her gun drawn as her eyes roved the room. "Is everything okay?"

"Yes. No. Put away the gun."

Karla nodded, but her posture didn't relax. "What's wrong?"

Charlotte hadn't realized how badly her hands were shaking until she tried to button her blouse. "The school is on fire."

Karla's eyes widened, and she backed toward the door. "I'll tell Joseph. We'll be ready to leave in two minutes."

Charlotte didn't bother to brush her hair or teeth. Karla and Joseph met her in the living room, and moments later they were speeding toward the school while questions bounced around in Charlotte's head. How had the fire started? How big was it? How bad was it?

She saw the flicker of orange flames against the inky black sky from half a mile away. Her heart constricted and her throat tightened in horror at the size of the flames.

This was bad. Really, really bad.

"Do you think it's the vandals?" Charlotte asked no one in particular.

"We'll launch a full investigation into the matter, Your Highness," Joseph promised.

The hotel's only fire truck was already at the scene, its hose spraying water toward the flames that licked up the front of the building. But the truck was small, intended for small blazes—not the roaring inferno that this fire appeared to be. It wouldn't be enough to put out the flame.

A night guard stood near the truck, his back a silhouette against the angry flames. Charlotte stumbled from the car, and the man turned. Luther. That was his name.

"Luther," she called. Charlotte could feel the heat of the flames, even from close to a hundred yards away. Large pieces of ash floated down from the sky while a harsh crackling, punctuated by the pops of embers, filled the air.

He walked quickly toward her, while the firefighters continued spraying water toward the flames. Shadows danced across Luther's face, making the harsh planes of his frown even more severe.

"Your Highness," he said. "Thank you for coming so quickly."

"What happened?"

Luther shook his head, running a hand through his hair. "We're still trying to figure that out. The alarms were tripped about an hour ago, but when we went to investigate, we didn't find anything. Figured it was an animal until we smelled the smoke."

This couldn't be happening. Charlotte swayed, feeling dizzy. Joseph reached out a hand, but Charlotte batted it away.

She couldn't collapse right now. Not while the school needed her.

"The hotel's two firefighters are doing all that they can," Luther said. "Bigger trucks from the city should be here within the hour. Until then, all we can do is pray the flames don't spread."

Charlotte shook her head violently, refusing to accept that answer. "I won't just stand here and do nothing."

Luther lifted his shoulders in a helpless shrug. "I'm not sure what we can do right now."

"There has to be something." Charlotte clutched her hands to her chest, watching the spidery fingers of the fire destroying her dream. Destroy the future of so many children. Water arced from the hose toward the building, wetting the roof.

"Why aren't they spraying the flames?" Charlotte asked.

"They're trying to keep the fire from spreading," Luther said. "It's our best move until the bigger trucks arrive."

"Of course!" Charlotte fumbled in her pockets, then realized she must have left her phone back in the hotel room. She turned to Joseph and Karla, resolve flowing through her. "Joseph, call Chief Mandla and tell him what's happening. Have him bring as many villagers as he can, as fast as possible. We'll form a water brigade and try to keep the fire from spreading. Karla, I want you to call the hotel and have them bring anything they have on hand to move water. Pitchers. Cups. Cleaning totes. I don't care. Tell them to send any employees that can be spared to help."

They both nodded and pulled out their phones while Charlotte headed toward the well at the back of the school.

They had to save the school. Failure wasn't an option. Not tonight.

It wasn't long before villagers and hotel employees began to arrive. Soon they had formed a line from the well to the school. Charlotte stood at the front of it, despite Joseph's protests, and tossed water on the partially bricked walls of the school until her arms ached.

But Charlotte didn't care that her muscles burned from the unfamiliar workout, or that her body was drenched in sweat from the heat of the flames. All she cared about was saving the school.

It felt like an eternity before the fire engines arrived from the city. They worked tirelessly throughout the night, but Charlotte knew the damage had already been done.

The school wouldn't open by September first. Not now.

Smoke stung her eyes, making them water and burn. *Where are you, Adam?* Charlotte silently cried as she tossed bucket after bucket of water. *You should be here, helping me.*

Dawn was just bathing the sky in a pink glow when the fire was finally extinguished. Charlotte stared at the charred front of the building, feeling as though her entire world had just exploded. The red bricks she'd imagined covered in ivy were now charred black. Sometime during the night the roof had collapsed, the wooden timbers unable to handle the power of the inferno. She was sure the interior was a total loss, although the fire inspector wouldn't let anyone inside to check.

Tears pooled in Charlotte's eyes as she thought of calling Adam and telling him about the fire. "At least no one was hurt," she whispered, wiping at her eyes.

Would he blame her for what had happened to the school tonight? She was supposed to have protected it while he was away.

Away with Brionna. Anger made her hands curl into fists, and Charlotte pressed them against her stomach, longing for the comfort of a good book. He should have been here. And—irrational though it was— she couldn't help wondering if maybe he could have saved the school.

Gravel crunched quietly underneath heavy feet, and Charlotte turned to see Chief Mandla walking toward her, his face lined with grief.

"I will find out who did this, Your Highness," he said, his tone severe. "And I will see that the guilty parties are brought to justice. That is a promise."

"It could have been an accident." Charlotte wiped again at her eyes. "The fire inspector's report will tell us for sure."

"I wish I could believe this was an accident." Chief Mandla's face was lined with guilt. "But this is the work of the boys I told you about, I'm certain."

"Maybe the damage isn't as bad as it appears." Charlotte rested a hand gently on the chief's arm. "Go home and get some rest. There's nothing more that we can do here tonight."

By the time Joseph and Karla convinced Charlotte to head back to the hotel, the sun had fully risen. But Charlotte knew she'd get no more rest tonight. The insurance company needed to be notified, the damage fully assessed, and action plan for rebuilding created.

Charlotte would have to call Adam and tell him what had happened.

Tears burned her eyes, and she brushed them away as she wandered into her bedroom. The phone lay forgotten on her bedspread, but Charlotte ignored it. She couldn't face Adam until she'd washed away the grime of the fire.

Charlotte took a long, hot shower, letting the tears run freely as she scrubbed her body clean. She fell into bed, reluctantly picking up her phone. Adam had to be notified. He needed to come home immediately, because Charlotte wasn't sure if the insurance company would even talk to anyone but him.

She reluctantly picked up the phone, swiping the screen awake.

A text icon blinked, and she opened it. Emma had texted again, but Charlotte ignored that text and opened Adam's instead.

Mr. Cartwright died a few hours ago.

Poor Brionna. Charlotte swallowed hard, not sure how to process this new information along with the grief of the fire. But death or no, Adam needed to come home. There were things Charlotte couldn't handle now—meetings with insurance adjusters, possible criminal charges filed against the perpetrators if caught. This was bigger than her.

She needed to hear Adam's voice.

Charlotte dialed the number, but it went straight to voice mail. She tried again with the same result.

She buried her face in the pillow, letting out a muffled yell. Why wasn't Adam answering his phone? What's more, why wasn't he here with her right now?

Brionna had her brothers. Right now, Charlotte had no one.

He'd been gone five days longer than promised. What did it say about their relationship, that Adam would rather help Brionna than help her?

"I'm an idiot," Charlotte mumbled.

The answer had been staring her in the face for days, but she hadn't wanted to believe the evidence. It was simple, really—Adam was with Brionna because he had stronger feelings for her than he did for Charlotte.

She glanced again at her phone, stomach churning. Gossip sites were wrong all the time. Adam had assured her that photo of him and Brionna holding hands meant nothing. But if it had, would he tell her the truth?

Charlotte swallowed hard and opened a web browser. Adam's texts and phone calls had grown less and less frequent over the past few days, and Charlotte had compensated by spending too much time on that stupid gossip site.

It didn't take long to find the evidence she needed. Charlotte's heart froze as she stared at the photo of Brionna in what could only be called lingerie, her lips pressed tightly against Adam's. He was clearly in pajamas too, his shirt stretched tightly across his biceps and feet bare.

Charlotte doubled over, her eyes blurred with tears. She tossed the phone away as though it were poison, gasping for breath.

The school was gone.

Adam was gone.

Her dreams had once again been crushed.

She rolled onto her side with a moan. What did it matter if the photo was just another paparazzo trying to twist the story to sell subscriptions? Facts didn't lie. Adam was in Boston with Brionna instead of in South Africa with her. Actions spoke louder than words, and it didn't get much clearer than that.

When Karla came in to check on Charlotte a few hours later, she said she wasn't feeling well and stayed in bed. Charlotte couldn't eat. Couldn't sleep. Didn't dare ask what was happening with the school.

She had failed on an epic scale, both professionally and romantically.

Emma called a few more times, but Charlotte let them all go to voice mail. At some point, Henry called, too, but Charlotte was crying again and didn't want to talk. She knew Emma was worried about her, and Henry's phone call meant Emma had probably confided her concerns in him. But talking to anyone felt pointless. They couldn't heal a broken heart anymore than Charlotte could.

Karla checked on Charlotte again, but she told her to go away. Had it been twelve hours since the fire? A day? Charlotte wasn't sure. All she knew was that Adam hadn't called.

Voices from the foyer floated into Charlotte's bedroom, and she burrowed deeper beneath the covers.

Her bedroom door slowly opened, and Charlotte blinked against the sudden light spilling in from the hallway.

Charlotte rose up on one elbow, blinking. "Henry?" He looked as handsome as ever in a perfectly pressed suit, his hair styled off his forehead.

"I'm not going to ask questions," he said quietly. "I just want you to come back to Durham with me. Will you do that, please?"

Home. She glanced at her phone, but the screen was still blank. Adam still hadn't called. Had Keith told him about the fire?

Charlotte wiped her eyes, nodding weakly. "Yes. Please, Henry. Take me home."

Chapter Twenty-Eight

Adam peered eagerly out the plane window as the craft dipped toward the ground in a slow but steady descent. He could just make out the scraggly tops of marula trees and the spotted giraffes feasting on their leaves, and his heart lept with joy at nearly being home.

He must have left his phone at the Cartwright Hotel in his rush to leave, because he hadn't been able to find it anywhere since boarding the plane. But that was okay—he'd just have to order in a new one. Right now, all that mattered was being with Charlotte. He couldn't wait to feel her arms around his neck. Longed to kiss her senseless.

Air whistled past the plane's wings, and then there was a thud as the wheels hit the ground. The plane taxied to a stop. A few yards away a black town car idled. Someone leaned against the door of the car, silhouetted by the sunlight. Adam's heart jumped with happiness until he realized that it was a man leaning against the sedan—Keith, not Charlotte.

The cabin door opened, and Adam loped down the stairs. Keith pushed away from the car and walked toward him, his face solemn.

Adam's steps faltered at his assistant's severe expression. "How did you know I was on my way?" Adam asked.

"I noticed that flight plans had been filed," Keith said. "Figured it had to be you returning from Boston, since your father is still in Dubai. I've been trying to reach you on your phone for hours."

"I accidentally left my cell back in Boston," Adam said slowly. Something was very, very wrong. He hadn't seen Keith this subdued since—well, since Mother's funeral.

Had something happened to Charlotte? Adam's heart thudded painfully in his chest, and he massaged it with one hand. He couldn't lose her. It would break him. If he'd been in Boston instead of here with Charlotte—

"Keith, what aren't you telling me?" Adam demanded.

"A lot." Keith held open the car door, motioning Adam inside. "We need to hurry back to the resort. I'll explain everything on the way."

Adam climbed into the car, feeling sick, and Keith got in behind him. When the sedan began cruising toward the hotel at speeds that Adam knew had to be illegal, his worry only grew.

"You'd better start talking," Adam said, giving Keith his full attention. "Is it Princess Charlotte?"

"What? No, Her Highness wasn't hurt. No one was, which we can count as a blessing." Keith pinched the bridge of his nose. "There's no real way to sugarcoat this. Last night, there was a fire at the school. The investigation is ongoing, but at this point it looks like arson. Chief Mandla thinks it was the boys who've been vandalizing the school."

Adam couldn't take in air. He leaned forward, hands on his knees, as he struggled to breathe.

A fire. The school had caught on fire. No, not caught—that implied an accident. Someone had set the school on fire.

"I was able to locate the insurance information and notify the company about the fire," Keith continued. "We won't have the final report for at least another twenty-four hours, but they're on alert to expect that information just as soon as we have it—"

"How bad is the damage?" Adam interrupted. He'd finally found his breath, but it hurt as it wheezed in and out of his chest. Charlotte must be a mess. That school was everything to her.

Keith was quiet, and Adam glanced over at him.

"How bad?" he demanded.

Keith sighed, rubbing his jaw. "The roof collapsed. Most of the interior is a total loss, and the front wall will probably need to be completely replaced, studs and all, since it's likely the structural integrity was compromised. Of course all the exterior brickwork was ruined, but we won't know the full extent of the damage until we can get the contractors in there to assess everything. The fire department has taped the entire area off until their investigation is finished."

Adam pushed a hand roughly through his hair, struggling to comprehend what he was hearing. Would he find anything more than charred rubble when he arrived at the school?

"How is Princess Charlotte handling this?" Adam asked. "She's put her heart and soul into the project. I can't imagine how she's feeling right now."

Keith's brow furrowed. "She didn't call you?"

Adam clenched his hand into a fist, struggling to hold his temper. "I lost my phone, remember?"

"Right. Prince Henry arrived just a few hours ago to take Her Highness back to Durham. They're probably halfway home by now. Something about a—"

Adam leaned forward and tapped the driver roughly on the shoulder. "Turn around," he demanded. "Head back to the airport. There's somewhere else I need to be."

"What?" Keith's eyes were wide, and his bewildered expression would have been comical if Adam's heart wasn't pounding in his chest at roughly five times its normal speed. "But the school. You need to—"

"I need to see Charlotte," Adam said.

"Her Highness?" Keith's tone was disbelieving. "Adam, I don't know if you fully understand the gravity of this situation. We need to petition the council for more time to open the school. This will add months to the project. There's no way we can open by—"

"I don't care about the school!" Adam practically yelled.

Keith's mouth fell open.

"I love Charlotte," Adam said. He should have been shouting that truth from the rooftops instead of skulking around in secret, like they had something to hide. "And I'm going after her. Please arrange for a new phone to be delivered to me in Durham. We'll keep in touch."

The plane ride to Durham, despite being half the length of the one from Boston, felt twice as long. All he could worry about for the entire flight was why Charlotte had left. Did some sort of family emergency necessitate her going back to Durham? He couldn't think of why else she would leave, especially after such a tragedy.

She loved that school. Only something truly awful would make her leave it so soon after the fire.

When the plane landed, Adam directed the driver to take him to the palace. He prayed his father's title would carry enough weight to grant him an audience with the princess, since no one knew they were—had been?—dating. Fresh fear coated Adam's tongue as he wondered if Charlotte was breaking up with him. Why else wouldn't she tell him she was leaving?

Maybe she had tried to call. If there was an emergency, she wouldn't wait for him to answer the phone before leaving.

When the town car pulled up to the guard shack, Adam handed over his identification and held his breath. Five minutes later, he was certain he'd be turned away. But then the guard motioned him forward, and they drove down the lane toward the private visitor's entrance of the palace.

Inside, Adam was directed to a small sitting room he'd never seen before. He'd been to the palace a few times throughout his life, but each had been for an official royal function held in one of the larger rooms of the palace. This room was definitely royal, with intricately carved crown moldings along the coffered ceiling and rich wood furniture accented by cream-and-silver striped fabric.

Adam sat on the edge of his chair, one leg bouncing nervously up and down. Would Charlotte even speak to him? Adam wasn't sure what had happened, but the pit in his stomach told him it was something he wouldn't like.

A rustle sounded at the doorway, and Adam rose as Charlotte entered. His heart flew into his throat as he took in her appearance. She wore a high-necked blouse with capped sleeves and a black skirt flowed around her calves. Her hair was pulled back in an elegant knot, and her makeup was perfectly done. But there was something about her eyes that set Adam on edge—a coldness he'd never seen there before.

Adam held out his arms, but when Charlotte made no move to walk toward him, he let them drop limply to his sides.

"What are you doing here, Adam?" she asked, her tone sharp.

Adam took a step toward her, unable to believe what he was hearing. "What do you mean, why am I here? I came to see you. What happened, Char? Why did you leave South Africa?"

She moved behind a chair, placing her hands on the furniture's curved back, as though needing to keep some distance between them. "Didn't you get my message about the school? You should be there right now."

Adam ran a hand through his hair, not understanding what was happening. "I left my phone in

Boston and haven't gotten a replacement yet. But Keith told me about the fire when I landed in South Africa."

Charlotte raised one eyebrow, her eyes—if possible—growing even colder. "And your response was to hop on a plane and come see me?"

"Of course." He took a step toward her, his heart aching when she took a step back.

Something was horribly, awfully wrong. And it wasn't just the fire.

"You should have stayed in South Africa." Charlotte looked down, running her hand over the back of the chair. "It isn't fair to leave this all on Keith's shoulders."

Adam took the chair gently from Charlotte's hands, moving it from between them. He put his hands on her shoulders, running them down her arms until he clutched her hands in his.

"Char," he whispered. "What is going on? Please, talk to me."

Her eyes were red, as though she'd been crying recently. He hadn't noticed that detail from across the room, or the dark circles underneath her eyes—she'd done a pretty good job of covering that up with makeup. But now he could see the exhaustion in her face, as though she hadn't slept in days.

Why had she been crying? Surely not over Mr. Cartwright's death. Adam didn't think the two of them had ever even met.

Charlotte pulled her hands from Adam's, and he reluctantly let them go. She withdrew a phone from a hidden pocket in her skirt and pulled something up on the screen, then handed it over to him.

Adam started at the photograph, bile rising in his throat. How had a reporter caught a photo of Brionna kissing him? He hadn't seen anyone else in the hallway, but it was clear from the angle that the picture had been taken before the door slammed shut behind Brionna.

"Char," Adam said. He sounded like a man drowning. "That isn't—"

"—what it looks like?" Charlotte finished. She took the phone back from him and dropped it in her pocket. "With the paparazzi, it never is. This isn't about the picture, Adam. It's about you staying in Boston with Brionna, instead of hurrying back to help me with the school."

Charlotte's words kept coming, the one-two of her verbal punches making him nauseous. "Brionna's dad was sick—"

"And the school was on fire!" Charlotte lifted a trembling hand to her lips, taking a deep breath. "You're more worried about disappointing Brionna than hurting me."

"That's not true." A single tear trailed down Charlotte's cheek, and the sight of it was nearly Adam's undoing. He ran his hands up and down her arms, desperate to make her understand. "Last night, I realized that I had my priorities all wrong. That's why I came back to South Africa, even though Mr. Cartwright had just died. I came back for *you*, Char. I want us to go public with our relationship. I'm done hiding. All I want is for us to be together."

Charlotte folded her arms, lips pressed into a firm line. "So you told Brionna about us?"

"Yes!"

Charlotte yanked her phone from her pocket, waving it back and forth in front of his face. "And then she . . . what? Put on some lingerie and tried to change your mind?"

Adam rubbed his eyes, bile rising in his throat.

He was losing Charlotte. He could feel it.

"I immediately pushed her away. That stupid kiss was never about me, Char. Brionna's dad had just—"

"You're still making excuses for her!" Charlotte threw her phone to the ground, where it landed with a crash. She brushed away her tears, shaking her head roughly back and forth. "This is why we can't be together, Adam. You're making excuses for Brionna instead of owning up to your mistakes. You're here, talking to me, instead of dealing with the fire in South Africa. I can't do this anymore."

Anger flowed through Adam, and he decided to let it flow. "Don't put this all on me. You've been looking for any excuse you can find to push me away again since the minute we got back together. You are so terrified of letting someone in that you'd rather sabotage your own happiness than take a risk on me."

Charlotte pointed an angry finger toward the door. "Get out."

"I'm willing to fight for us, Char. Because I think we're worth that. Are you willing to do the same?"

"Adam, you don't even know what you're fighting for. You don't know what you want!" She folded her arms, glaring. "You wanted Brionna because your mother thought it was best for you. Then you wanted the school, because your father gave you the project. Now you've abandoned Brionna and the school because you think you want me."

"I love you." Adam's voice cracked, and he blinked quickly. "Please don't do this."

Silence stretched between them, and for a moment, Adam dared hope. Then Charlotte's eyes hardened, and she took a step back.

"It's over, Adam. Go back to South Africa and try to salvage the school project. I can't be a part of it anymore."

"Please—"

He grasped for her hand, but she wrenched it from his grip, head shaking violently.

"I'm sorry," she whispered.

And then she disappeared from the room.

Chapter Twenty-Nine

Charlotte walked into her suite of rooms, exhausted from a long day spent doing story time at the Castlebridge Library. But it was a good, satisfying kind of exhaustion. She'd implemented a city-wide literacy program after returning to Durham, and today she'd turned the program over to someone else. Over the past three months, the children had taught Charlotte to be honest with herself, and she loved them for it. But it was time to move on.

She tucked today's reading selection under one arm—a playful picture book about a cheetah who lived on the African safari, but was afraid to see how fast he could run. Charlotte had written it herself and received the first copy from her publisher just last week. The children had loved the story, and it had healed a part of her soul to see them connect with the story. She'd poured her heart into the book, and in return experienced a lot of personal realizations and healing.

The last three months had been brutal. Adam's words had echoed in Charlotte's head every moment of every day until she knew that he was right. And that knowledge—that she had sabotaged their relationship, however unintentionally—hurt almost as much as the breakup itself.

Charlotte could finally admit that she had looked for excuses to push Adam away. Had never allowed herself to trust him completely.

The fire hadn't been Adam's fault, and he'd only tried to be a good friend by staying in Boston with Brionna. Charlotte also knew he was telling the truth about the kiss, because she knew Adam. He was a good man. One she missed terribly.

Adam had made some poor decisions, of that there was no doubt. But so had Charlotte. She hadn't clearly voiced her concerns, especially over his long stay in Boston. Hadn't been vocal enough with her own opinions. But her biggest regret of all was refusing to fight for their relationship. She could only hope that Adam would give her a second chance.

Charlotte kicked off her heels and ran a finger along the letter tucked carefully in her sash. She must have written twelve drafts of the stupid thing, but she finally had a version she wanted to give him.

Tomorrow, she'd fly to South Africa and beg for Adam's forgiveness. She had run when she should have stayed and fought. But Charlotte was finally ready to make the right choice.

She was ready to fight for Adam.

Charlotte reached up, pulling the pins out of her hair as she called, "Becky, is there anything else on today's schedule? I hope not, because I've still got some packing to do, and I'm exhausted—"

She entered the living room and came to an abrupt halt, her eyes going immediately to the man standing in front of her fireplace, the mantle nearly as tall as him.

"Hi," he said, his low voice sending shivers up her spine. She hadn't heard that voice in three long months.

"Adam," Charlotte breathed. She pulled the picture book closer to her chest, the rapid beat of her heart thrumming against the cover.

He shoved his hands in his pockets, looking uncertain. His crooked smile turned her knees to water. "I thought about calling first, but I was worried you'd kick me out."

"How did you get in here?" Charlotte looked for Joseph and Karla, but they'd made themselves scarce.

"Emma, if you can believe it." Adam lifted his shoulders in a shrug. "I don't know why she decided to help me, but I'm grateful to her for it."

Charlotte set the book on an end table, taking another cautious step toward Adam. "She's probably tired of listening to me cry about how much I miss you."

"You've missed me?"

"Every single day." Charlotte hurried across the room, very aware of her bare feet and messy hair. "I'm so sorry about the awful things I said to you. I was completely out of line, and even worse, I was wrong."

Adam met her halfway, and suddenly they were a mere foot apart from each other. She could smell the spicy scent of his aftershave, and it was making it hard to think.

He was here, right in front of her. What did this mean?

"No, you were absolutely right." Adam ran a hand through his hair, then over his jaw. "When I left, I was so angry. I had put my heart on the line, and you told me that I wasn't ready to give it to you."

"Adam—"

He lifted a finger, setting it gently against her lips. She inhaled sharply, her entire body tingling with the contact.

"And you were right. By the time I landed once again in South Africa, I had realized that I didn't deserve you. Not yet. So I've spent the past three months doing everything I can to be worthy of your love."

"Oh, Adam." Charlotte took his hand in both of hers, hope flaring when he didn't pull away. She cradled it against her cheek, taking a step closer to him. "You were the one who was right. I was so terrified of being in a real relationship that I pushed you away. I didn't know how to be open or vulnerable or even honest with myself. But I've spent the past three months working on it."

Adam shook his head, moving his hand to the back of her neck. "You have nothing to work on. You're perfect just the way you are."

Tears blurred Charlotte's eyes, and she blinked them away quickly. His hand was massaging the back of her neck, sending explosions of heat across her entire body.

"I am so, so sorry for not putting your needs first, Char. I should have been there for you when the fire happened. I can't imagine what watching the school burn felt like."

"Probably not any worse than being forced to relive your mother's death while watching Mr. Cartwright die. I should have been more understanding about your time in Boston."

His mouth quirked up in a grin. "So we're both sorry for our mistakes?"

She nodded.

"Then can we agree to start over?"

Charlotte bit her lip, resting her hands on his biceps. "I don't want to start over. I'd much rather pick up right where we left off."

Adam took a step back, and Charlotte's hands dropped to her sides. She blinked, disoriented, as Adam walked to the fireplace mantle and picked up a thin folder she hadn't realized was resting there.

He walked back to her, handing over the folder. "Here. There's something I want to show you."

Charlotte accepted it cautiously, not sure if this was a good or bad thing. "What's this?"

"Open it."

Charlotte stared at Adam, but his expression was unreadable. She slid a nail underneath the flap and pulled out an email, then scanned it quickly.

"Why are you showing me an email between you and Hudson Cartwright?" It looked like Hudson was asking some questions about properties in South Africa, and Adam was answering them.

"Because I wanted to show you that I've learned from my mistakes. The Cartwrights are still friends, and I've been helping them in any way I can since Mr. Cartwright's passing. But I make sure all communication is through either Hudson, Mason, or Ethan. I haven't spoken to Brionna since leaving Boston."

He'd given up Brionna for her. Charlotte clutched the folder to her chest, heart beating rapidly. "Did you do this for me?"

"Absolutely." Adam's eyes were smoldering with a fire she'd never seen there before, and it made her heart jump erratically. "Because love means putting your partner's needs first, no matter what. If that means no longer talking to Brionna, well, it's a small price to pay for your forgiveness." A smile quirked the corner of his mouth. "We weren't really that close, anyway."

Could he possibly still love her? Charlotte bit her lip, hope taking flight in her chest.

Adam motioned again to the folder. "Keep going. There's more."

Charlotte pulled out the rest of the papers and froze. Sitting on top was a picture of the school—one she recognized, and yet it looked somehow different. The brick was redder than before, the trim around the doors and windows a little whiter.

"We've had crews working around the clock to repair the damage," Adam said softly. "The council extended the deadline by six months, and we're on track to open the first week of January. Chief Mandla convinced me to press charges against the boys who set the fire, and we haven't had any problems with vandalism since."

"You've done all this work in just three months?"

Charlotte flipped through the pages, taking in the freshly painted walls, the newly repaired roof, the brand new floor. How had they accomplished so much in such a short period of time?

"It's your dream, Char," Adam said quietly. "I wasn't about to let it die."

Charlotte flipped to the last page. It was a close-up of the sign hung above the front door, the school name etched in white stone.

But it didn't say the School Montgomery.

She ran trembling fingers over the words, unable to believe what she was reading. *The Princess Charlotte Academy of Learning.*

The papers tumbled to the ground, and Charlotte's eyes flew up to meet Adam's. "You named the school after me?"

"It was the only name that made sense." Adam's arm slid around her waist, pulling her slowly closer. Her entire body tingled with the contact, and she felt simultaneously giddy and light-headed. "After all, the school never would have been possible without your help."

Her eyes pooled with tears, and she blinked quickly, staring at the picture that had fluttered to the floor.

"I can't believe you did that. I was so horrible to you."

"No, you were hurt. And that was my fault." His knuckles trailed against her cheek, then brushed her hair behind one ear. She'd kept it blonde these past few months, deciding the color suited her. "I love you so much, Charlotte. And I will do anything to prove that to you. Tell me—what do you need from me? Because I will do anything to win back your trust."

"Oh, Adam." She slid her hands up his chest, then locked them behind his neck. "I love you, too. You don't have to win me back, because my heart has always been yours. I'm yours."

He crushed her to him, and then his lips were on hers, kissing her breathless. Charlotte cradled his face in her hands, relishing the feel of his beard against her palms. She gasped as his kiss deepened while his arms pulled her impossibly closer.

At long last he pulled away, resting his forehead against hers.

"No secrets this time," he said. "I want the entire world to know that I love you completely."

She laughed, reaching into her sash and withdrawing the letter. "That's pretty much what I said—that I'm sorry, that I love you, and that I want us to be together forever."

He took the letter, his brows furrowing. "What's this?"

"A letter. I was going to give it to you tomorrow. In South Africa."

His eyes widened, meeting hers once more. "You were coming to South Africa?"

"I thought it was about time I finished what I started—with our relationship, and with the school."

Adam laughed, kissing her deeply once more. "Third time's a charm?"

321

"It better be."

"It will be," he countered.

He tucked the letter in his breast coat pocket, then lowered his head to hers once more. And Charlotte knew that for the first time in her life, she was truly home to stay.

Epilogue

Charlotte held the pair of scissors poised over the red ribbon, Adam's hand on hers, as they smiled for the camera.

She couldn't believe this day was finally here—the grand opening of the school. For a while, she'd wondered if it would ever happen.

The photographer clicked away on her camera, and Adam's lips brushed Charlotte's ear as he murmured, "Ready?"

"Ready," she whispered.

They sliced through the red ribbon together, and excited clapping echoed on the clear January breeze. The local tribesmen were all in animal-skin robes, shivering against the cooler winter temperature, but it felt like a pleasantly warm day to Charlotte after spending the last two weeks in the freezing winter rains peppering Durham.

The last few months had been wonderful and challenging and rewarding. She and Adam had worked together on the school. They had argued and made up and kissed and laughed and learned new things about each other—sometimes while in the same country, and sometimes over the phone while Charlotte saw to business in Durham.

The ends of the ribbon fluttered in the breeze as tribesmen broke out in a celebratory dance. Charlotte clasped her hands together, Adam's arm around her shoulders as happiness flowed through her.

There were still members of the tribe who didn't want to send their children to the school, and that was okay. But with the arrest of the boys, the vandalism had finally stopped. The parents of the teens had been deeply shamed by their sons' actions, but Adam had pled with the judge for leniency and soon the boys would be released from jail. Best of all, without the constant setbacks, the rest of the school's construction had gone relatively smoothly.

Charlotte had never worked harder for something in her life, and she'd never found the end result more rewarding.

Chief Mandla walked up the steps of the school, offering his hand to Adam. The two men shared a warm shake, and the chief looked back and forth between them with tears glistening in his eyes.

"I cannot thank the two of you enough for this," he said. "You are blessing generations to come with your selfless efforts."

"Thank you for allowing us to be a part of this." Charlotte blinked quickly, fighting the emotions that were suddenly overwhelming her. "Helping with this school has truly been a dream come true for me."

"And it helped me win back the princess." Adam dropped a kiss on Charlotte's cheek, and she leaned into him. With Alex and Stefan married, and Henry officially engaged, Charlotte and Adam's relationship was all over the papers now. But for the first time in her life, she could truly say she didn't care.

The next few hours were a joyous celebration of the school's opening. On Monday, they'd hold their first official day of class. Charlotte knew the new headmaster and teachers would do a wonderful job, but she hoped she'd be able to at least peek in on a few of the classes and see the results of their hard work.

Eventually, the reporters headed back to their rooms at the hotel, and the locals went back to the village to sleep. But Adam and Charlotte sat on the stairs in the lobby of the school, enjoying the quiet after a long day of activity.

"I can't believe it's really over," Charlotte said. The hard marble of the stairs was hurting her backside, but she didn't want this moment to ever end. She looked around the school, her eyes lingering on the paintings hung along one wall. They'd held a contest for the school children and given the winning pieces a place of honor in the foyer.

Adam pulled Charlotte against his side, and she nestled into him, leaning her head on his shoulder. "This is but the first of many projects we'll embark on together, my love."

She raised one eyebrow, looking up at him. "Oh? Do you have something specific in mind?"

"In fact, I do." Adam reached into his pocket and withdrew an envelope, handing it over. "Nothing is set in stone, but I thought this might be a good starting place for us."

Charlotte took the envelope, her curiosity piqued. She slid a finger underneath the flap and pulled out the paper.

Her eyes clouded over, obscuring the words. She stared up at Adam, hardly able to believe what she was reading.

"Are you serious?" she asked.

Adam nodded, brushing a strand of her hair behind one ear. "I know how much you've enjoyed working with the children in Durham, and I thought an after-school literacy program would be perfect for us—sort of an expansion of what you've done with the

Castlebridge Library. I've already chosen a few possibilities for the land. We can go look at them and choose a location together."

"But . . . what about the Hotel Montgomery? Your life is in South Africa. A program like this will be a lot of work."

"Which is precisely why I want to make Durham my full-time home once more. My life is wherever you are, Char." Adam took her hands tightly in both of his, and the paper fell forgotten to the floor. "I've spoken to my father, and he agrees that there will need to be a transition period as we hire and train a new manager for the property here. But we've spoken with the manager of the hotel in downtown Castlebridge, and he's interested in a swap. It seems his wife is keen on escaping the hustle of the city, and an African adventure seems to be just the thing she's looking for."

"Oh, Adam . . ." Charlotte's heart pounded furiously in her chest. "This is a big step for our relationship. Are you sure you're willing to move back to Durham for me?"

"I'm willing to do a lot more than that."

Slowly, Adam dropped to the school floor. Her position on the stairs put them almost at eye level with each other. Adam reached into his suit coat pocket and withdrew a ring box.

Charlotte's hand flew to her mouth as she gasped.

"I love you more than this hotel, more than the school, more than South Africa. And I will willingly follow you anywhere in the world, if you'll let me." He flipped open the box, and Charlotte stared at the giant solitaire diamond nestled in a plain gold band. "I don't ever want to be apart from you. Charlotte, will you do me the honor of becoming my wife?"

Charlotte nodded furiously, throwing herself at Adam. He caught her with a laugh and they both tumbled to the floor. Charlotte took his face between her hands, kissing him soundly.

"Can I take that as a yes?" Adam asked with a chuckle.

"Yes! Yes, I will marry you."

"Good." Adam slipped the ring onto Charlotte's finger, kissing her knuckle just above the symbol of their love.

"Are you sure about moving back to Durham?" Charlotte asked, staring in awe at the ring. "We could possibly stay in South Africa, at least for a few years."

"I want to come back to Durham. Your family is there, and right now, it makes the most sense for us to be near them. Alex and Libby will be announcing her pregnancy any day now, and you'll want to be close by to watch your little niece or nephew grow up."

"But what if we miss South Africa?"

Alex grinned. "Then we'll come back and visit frequently."

Charlotte knew he was right, but her heart already ached at the thought of leaving the azure blue skies and breathtaking savannas of South Africa behind. "Maybe one day it will make sense to make living here a permanent arrangement."

"Maybe," Adam agreed. "But it doesn't matter to me where we are, as long as we're together."

Charlotte took Adam's chin firmly in her hands and whispered fervently, "I love you, Adam Montgomery."

"I love you too, Your Highness." He gave her a devilish grin. "There's no getting rid of me this time."

"No more winning back the princess," she agreed, giving him a light kiss. "You've won me forever this time. And I'm eternally grateful that you did."

"Let's not make it a long engagement," Adam said. "I don't want to wait another moment to start our lives together."

Charlotte gave a happy sigh, wrapping her arms around him tightly. "Mr. Montgomery, that is perhaps the most romantic thing you've ever said to me. I absolutely agree."

And she knew that whatever the future held, it would be okay. Because she'd get to face that future with Adam at her side.

About the Author

LINDZEE ARMSTRONG is the *USA Today* bestselling author of the No Match for Love series, Royal Secrets series, Kiss Me series, and Chasing Tomorrow series. In case it wasn't obvious, she's always had a soft spot for love stories. In third grade, she started secretly reading romance novels, hiding the covers so no  one would know (because hello, embarrassing!), and dreaming of her own Prince Charming.

Lindzee met her true love while at college, where she graduated with a bachelor's in history education. They are now happily married and raising twin boys in the Rocky Mountains.

Like any true romantic, Lindzee loves chick flicks, ice cream, and chocolate. She believes in sigh-worthy kisses and happily ever afters, and loves expressing that through her writing.

To find out about future releases, you can join Lindzee's reader's club by visiting her website, www.LindzeeArmstrong.com.

If you enjoyed this book, please take a few minutes and leave a review. This is the best way you can say thank you to an author! It really helps other readers discover books they might enjoy. Thank you!

CPSIA information can be obtained
at www.ICGtesting.com
Printed in the USA
LVHW051608200820
663741LV00011B/903